FROM HERE ON OUT HIS GUN WOULD DO THE TALKING. . . .

Pearly urged him to get out while the getting was good, but Sam Teacher would have none of it. True, there was a bounty on his head, signed by the U.S. Commissioner himself . . . and it was also true that cattle baron Matt Drury would pay good money to see him dead.

Sam Teacher was no fool—he knew the odds, and what he was up against. But he'd sworn vengeance upon Santee Bales, and that was a score he'd settle no matter what the risk. Because in the end Sam knew, as he had always known, that it would come to this—man against man, one gun each, and one of them dead when the dust finally cleared.

Luke Short Novels:

Bold Rider
Bounty Guns
Brand of Empire
The Branded Man
King Colt
The Man on the Blue
Marauders' Moon
Raw Land
Savage Range

BOUGHT WITH A GUN

(formerly titled *Gun Bought Grant*)

LUKE SHORT

A DELL BOOK

Published by
Dell Publishing
a division of
Bantam Doubleday Dell Publishing Group, Inc.
666 Fifth Avenue
New York, New York 10103

ISBN: 0-440-10744-X

Reprinted by arrangement with The Estate of
Frederick D. Glidden

Printed in the United States of America

Published simultaneously in Canada

New Dell Edition

April 1989

10 9 8 7 6 5 4 3

KRI

BOUGHT

WITH

A GUN

CHAPTER ONE

THE PLAZA OF SANTA LUZ was flanked on three sides by wooden-awninged stores. Only three things distinguished it from its sister towns of the Territory: it was the capital; it had a Governor's Palace that made up the fourth side of the plaza; and it had six good saloons on the other three sides.

In a back room of the second best, a man was interrupted at an afternoon glass of beer by the entrance of a puncher. The seated man's shoulders were nearly as thick as they were broad, but his head was curiously small. His face was tightly drawn. Under its swart skin every tiny muscle was visible, like the face of a man who has been flayed. His dark eyes were bland and cunning and merciless, not eyes that went with the clothes he wore—those of a working puncher. He was asking all the questions, while the other man, tall and dusty, was answering them.

"Who did Teacher ride in with, Rhodes?"

"Bohannon, from over at the marshal's office."

"That doesn't make sense."

"Not any."

"Are you sure?"

"I saw him, I tell you."

"Was he armed?"

"Same as always. Two guns."

"Then what?"

"Bohannon left him at the Exchange House."

"To sleep?"

"Yeah. He's there now."

"Asleep?"

"I made sure. I could hear him through the room door."

"How was he dressed?"

"Blue-checked shirt, Levi's, flat-crowned black Stetson, and vest."

"And he came in with a marshal?"

"Unh-hunh."

A pause.

"Could he get out of that room without being seen?"

"Sure. His window opens onto a store roof."

"Well, well."

The order of questioning was now reversed. The puncher, Rhodes, asked the questions, and the other man answered them.

"Want me to make a try for him, chief?"

"Don't be a fool."

"Since when did he start riding around with a marshal, and him with a price on his head?"

"Think a minute."

"I am. Why is he?"

"The Governor wants him, or the Commissioner, I suppose."

"Sure they do. About five thousand dollars' worth, ain't it?"

"Not for the reward money, or he wouldn't have been armed."

"He's still a wanted man, ain't he?"

"Technically. He won't be long, if he rode in with a marshal."

"What do you aim to do?"

"Plenty. I want the Runt."

"He's half drunk, out front. What for?"

"Go buy a blue-checked shirt, a black flat-brimmed Stetson, and a red bandanna. His size. Then bring them back here to me."

He seemed to be asleep, but even as the sound of footsteps swelled in the corridor outside, his hand, which had been fisted on the pillow, unfisted and slid underneath it.

When the knock came, he pushed himself up on an elbow and called, "What do you want?"

"There's a man to see you," the clerk's voice came through the door.

"Send him away."

"He's here now. Right here."

"Send him away, I said." While he was talking, he slid off the bed. Erect, without his shirt, he was undersize. His chest and shoulders were solid and beautifully knit without being heavy. His face, wholly awake now, was tough, arrogant beneath his tow-colored hair. Silently he moved over against the wall, looking not at the door but at the window.

The knock came again.

"Get away from here," he said gently.

Another voice spoke then: *"Amigo Sam!"*

His head swiveled toward the door and he walked over to it, removing the chair and opening the door. To the clerk he said, "Drag it," and to the other man, a browned Mexican of middle years in sun-faded tatters, he put out a hand and smiled.

"Como 'sta, amigo." In Spanish he continued: "Come in."

The Mexican, pulling off his hat, stepped inside. He smiled, too, as if courtesy were fully as urgent as what he was about to say.

"He is here, Sam."

"Who?"

"That *cabron,* Santee Bales. I have seen him."

"No! Where?"

"At the Paradise. He is fighting."

"Why?"

"He is drunk."

Sam's forehead wrinkled a little as he stared at the Mexican. "You have seen it?"

"I have seen it."

While the Mexican waited, Sam snatched up a checkered shirt, put it on, and strapped on his gun belt. Afterward they left, Sam leading.

They walked through the lobby out onto the hotel's awninged porch. Squinting against the sunlight that poured down onto the hard-baked adobe of the plaza, Sam saw that the square was slowly emptying toward the Paradise saloon. His eyes narrowed a little, suspicious, and without moving his head his glance traveled toward the bank across the plaza.

"He was never drunk in his life," he murmured to the Mexican.

He had no sooner finished saying it than a man stepped out of the bank. He was carrying a tow-sack. He was dressed in a blue-checked shirt, a black flat-brimmed Stetson, and Levi's. A red bandanna was either shading the lower part of his face or seemed to be; the man had his head down and it was hard to tell.

"Ah," the small man said. His glance hauled away from the man at the bank and pulled up closer to scan the line of horses at the tie rail in front of the hotel porch. Then he vaulted the low porch railing, dodged under the tie rail, drew out a carbine from a saddle boot, vaulted back over the railing to the cool depths of the porch, and stopped beside one of the porch pillars.

"Sam, be careful!" the Mexican said.

"It is all right, *amigo,*" Sam murmured. He took a deliberate rest against the pillar and hauled the carbine up. A bystander, who had been watching this, stared at Sam from the top step.

"Move," Sam said.

The man dropped to a sitting position, his head swiveled to look across the plaza. The man in the checkered shirt was on a horse now, and he was cantering down the street. He swerved for a freight wagon, touched spurs to his horse, and turned right at the corner.

At the moment, Sam shot. It was a good hundred yards distant, over the heads of teams and saddle horses at the tie rails. Still, the man in the checked shirt dropped from his horse.

At the shot, the men who were heading for the Paradise stopped and looked around. Someone on the far corner yelled. A man in the crowd yelled back, and then the tide of movement headed for the downed man in the checkered shirt.

Sam grinned and let the carbine slack off. "All right," he said to the man on the steps. "You can get up."

He was about to turn when he felt the warm barrel of a gun jammed against his back. He did not move, only said, "Take that out of there."

It pulled away, and he turned around to confront an army lieutenant.

"That was murder if I ever saw it," the lieutenant said angrily.

"Let's go see if it was," Sam said.

Still carrying the carbine, he marched down the steps ahead of the lieutenant. Things were happening now. Two men boiled out of the bank, yelling at the top of their lungs. Men on the street started to run. The whole crowd that had been choking the Paradise now backwashed and started to flow in a ragged stream across the plaza.

The crowd had already formed when the army lieutenant demanded way for himself and Sam. They pulled up at the inside edge of a cleared circle. The man in the checkered shirt was being rolled over on his back by a man with a star on his vest. The deputy straightened up at the appearance of the lieutenant. He looked once at the lieutenant and then at his prisoner and said, "You've just made yourself five thousand dollars, lieutenant, if you can get that gun out of his hands before he kills you." He had pulled his own gun while he was talking and he leveled it at Sam.

Sam dropped the carbine in the dirt. "Look in the tow-sack, you knothead," he said in a mild voice.

The deputy didn't move. He said, "Look in it, someone," and kept his eyes on the small man.

"It's money," an investigator announced. "A lot of money."

The circle of watchers was broken again, this time to let in a heavy man in a black coat. He took one look at the sack and walked over and squatted behind it.

"This is it," he announced. "This man stuck up the bank."

Sam grinned. His glance traveled the crowd circling him. There were more people watching him than were watching the money, the banker, or the robber, who was hurt but not dead.

His glance came to rest on a tall, smiling man, a man whose shoulders were as thick as they were wide.

"Hello, Santee," he said.

"Hello, Sam," the man answered.

"Sober now?"

"Sure. I'm scared sober," Santee murmured. They were smiling at each other the way two wary dogs wag their tails on the circle before the fight starts.

The deputy said, "Now wait a minute. What happened?"

Sam didn't look at him. He was watching Santee Bales.

"Nice shot," Santee said.

"A hard target, a small target," Sam said. "Why was he small, Santee?"

Santee shrugged. "All runts think they're tough."

"Why did he have on a checked shirt, Santee?"

"Maybe the dance-hall girls like that kind."

"Why did he have on a black hat, Santee?"

"To keep his half pint of brains from drying up, I suppose."

"Listen," the deputy said in a hard voice. "What's going on here?"

Sam looked at him with mild interest. "Shut up," he said. His glance returned to Santee.

"Know the man, Santee?" he asked.

Santee shook his head, still smiling, and answered, "When I first looked at him, I thought it was you."

"All right," the deputy said. "Put out your hands, Teacher."

Sam Teacher put out his hands. The name seemed to electrify the crowd, raising a loud murmur of talk.

A newcomer, wearing the uniform of a high-ranking army officer, broke through the crowd and came over to the deputy.

"The Commissioner wants to see that man," he said quietly to the deputy.

"Who?"

"The United States Commissioner."

"But it's Sam Teacher, the outlaw!"

"I know."

The deputy looked at him. "All right, it's your funeral. Got a squad of your men to guard him?"

"He'll come, all right," the army man said. "Take off those handcuffs, too."

CHAPTER TWO

"THE TROUBLE WITH RELIGION," the U.S. Commissioner said sourly, "is that it doesn't provide for exceptions like you. If I turn my other cheek, you'll smack it off."

"That's right."

The Commissioner regarded the man across the sleek mahogany desk with a thoroughly wry expression. As a poor boy, the Commissioner had known abuse; as a cowhand he had felt iron authority; as a lawyer he had learned defeat and humility; as a big rancher he had known the pleasures and sorrows of gambling; and as United States Commissioner he had experienced the woes of high office. It seemed to him now that none of these hardships had taught him patience, the thing he most needed when face to face with this unsmiling, casual, arrogant, undersized outlaw who sat across from him—Sam Teacher by name.

The Commissioner got a firm grasp on his temper and shifted a little in his chair. It wasn't his chair really; this room in the Palace of the Governor had been loaned to him for the occasion by the Governor himself.

"Apparently," he began again, "gratitude isn't listed among your virtues."

"No."

"It doesn't mean anything to you that the Governor will wipe out all the charges you've managed to accumulate in twenty-two years? It doesn't—"

"One," Teacher said.

"It doesn't—" The Commissioner paused. "What?"

"One."

"One what?"

"Twenty-one years. Go on."

The Commissioner did not hide his exasperation this time. He leaned across the table. "I say, besides the ten thousand dollars that will be yours for the job, you don't think it worth while to have—to have"—here he paused and consulted the paper that the Governor's secretary had prepared for him—"seven murder charges, eighteen robbery-with-deadly-weapon charges, not to mention this shooting in the plaza this afternoon and several dozen other charges ranging from assault and battery to inciting to riot—you don't think it worth while to have all those dropped?"

"No."

The Commissioner blinked. "Why not?"

Towheaded Sam Teacher was in the act of rolling a smoke, but his hard blue eyes were directed at the Commissioner, and they held a kind of bland, caustic mockery strangely appropriate to a face that was young, less than full, unlined but weather-burned. It wore an innocence overlaid with skepticism, and flaunted a hard-bought, shrewd pride that was visible in the line of the jaw, the straight nose—and the smile.

"They're bogus, most of them," he said.

He touched a match to his cigarette and threw the match over his shoulder without noticing that it landed on the deep-piled carpet. He put a leg up over the arm of the oversize chair and scratched the back of his head with his thumb. "Come on, Pop. Let's talk money."

"How much?"

"Twenty-five thousand."

"But the Governor is giving you a pardon!" the Commissioner said. "That can't be counted in money."

"That's the trouble."

"He won't listen to twenty-five thousand. After all, that money has to be accounted for."

"Okay." The leg came down. "I think I'll drift."

"Now wait," the Commissioner said hastily. "Consider the job, Teacher. It isn't much. Matt Drury owns that whole corner of the Territory. On his land is the only mountain pass through which the Southwestern and Rio Grande can come into the country, and they've got to have a right-of-way in forty days. Matt Drury won't give it to them and if they don't get it they'll keep going west and miss the whole central part of the Territory. Short of bribery, which wouldn't interest Matt Drury, and short of murder, which you'll be punished for, you have forty days to persuade Matt Drury to give the railroad a right-of-way through that canyon. And you'll get ten thousand dollars. And you'll get a pardon."

Sam Teacher yawned. "You through?"

"Yes."

"Then I'll drift."

He rose, and the Commissioner rose with him. "Sit down," the Commissioner said wearily. "I'll put your proposition before the Governor. He'll refuse, of course."

"He'll take it," Teacher said idly.

The Commissioner paused and asked, "What makes you think he'll submit to this holdup?"

Sam Teacher stared at this man who was old enough to be his grandfather. Then he looked away, bored. "Politics," he said.

"You'd never give a man in public office the credit for doing an unselfish thing, would you, Teacher?" the Commissioner asked sternly.

"No."

"And getting a railroad down here, a railroad that means the very lifeline of this Territory—that's petty politics, too."

"Unh-hunh."

The Commissioner said quietly, "You're criminally wrong."

Teacher looked over at him again and looked away. Then he swiveled his head and leaned forward in his chair. "Listen, Pop. Drury likes the Governor and hates railroads. The Governor likes Drury and he likes the railroad. What does that shake down to?"

"I don't follow your reasoning."

"All right. The Governor needs Matt Drury's money for the next campaign. He needs the railroad to get votes. If he gets both he's Governor again."

"Simple as that, eh?"

Teacher leaned back. "To me, sure. It'll just cost him twenty-five thousand dollars, is all."

The Commissioner left the room without another word. Teacher remained in his chair a few moments, then, becoming restless, he rose and started to walk about the room. Against the iron law forbidding the wearing of guns in the Governor's Palace, he had a six-gun strapped to his hip. It looked oversize against his slim waist, and when his hand hung beside it, as it almost always did, it looked too small to fit that gun.

He stopped now in front of a gloomy oil portrait, one of six that lined the walls of the room. It was the likeness of a former Governor, one of the sons of the Spanish colonists, and it exhibited a heavy, smooth-shaven face. Teacher fought down the impulse to draw a mustache on it, and went on to the others. Then he paused at the window, then turned away and sat down at the desk. He was about to put his feet up on it when he saw a rectangular box of inlaid wood among the papers on the desk top.

It was a box of cigars. He lighted one, took a dozen trial puffs, and made a wry face. Then he put the cigar, still burning, back in the humidor and sat back in the chair. Boredom relaxed his face.

He looked at the desk top then, noting idly that his boots were resting on some official-looking papers. His attention was attracted to a miniature elk's head of gilded metal, in the neck of which was a small desk clock. It rested in the exact center and rear of the flat-topped desk, and the antlers lifted above the head in a thin, graceful sweep. Sam Teacher studied it for some time, then his glance shifted to some thick rubber bands lying near it. Unconsciously, then, his glance lifted to the picture of the Spanish Governor on the far wall.

Interest flickered in his eyes. His feet came down and he reached for the clock. It was heavy, he found, when he lifted it over in front of him. He reached for one of the rubber bands and interlaced it among the antlers. He drew it back in a test trial and found it satisfactorily elastic. Picking up one of the pens that lay racked in front of the inkwell, he laid it in the crotch of the antlers. Drawing back his rubber band and fitting the tip of the pen in it, he aimed the point at the portrait across the room.

It was a nice question of sighting, he soon saw—so much so that he kicked the chair away from him, got down on his knees, and squinted along the pen.

The U.S. Commissioner found him this way, kneeling behind the desk, eye squinted along the pen that lay in the crotch of the antlers, one hand drawing back the rubber band of the makeshift slingshot.

"Quiet," Teacher said.

There was a breathless moment, during which the Commissioner paused, a look of bewilderment on his face. Then the *zung* of the released rubber band sang out, and a split second later there was a hollow booming sound across the room, as if the side of a cardboard carton had been thumped. The Commissioner looked across the room. The pen protruded from the left eye of Don Rafael Arturo Ulibarri y Perez y Mudarra.

Teacher rose to his feet, his hands on his hips, a faint smile on his face. "I figured it was heavier," he said.

The Commissioner's face was a study. Disbelief gave way to anger, and for a moment it remained there, inarticulate, and then resignation flooded over it, and he sighed.

"The Governor didn't object," the Commissioner said stiffly.

Teacher was still looking at the portrait. "Why should he?"

"There are several things I want understood first," the Commissioner said. He hauled the chair back to the desk and sat down, and Teacher lounged on the arm of the other chair.

"In the first place," the Commissioner began, "there's a stockmen's meeting here at Santa Luz this week. My advice would be for you to stay hidden until dark and then ride out of town. Especially after that shooting this afternoon."

"Why?"

"There's a stockmen's bounty of ten dollars for wolves, twenty-five dollars for mountain lion, and five thousand for Sam Teacher," the Commissioner said dryly. "Of course, that's void now, but some of them might forget."

"What else?" Teacher drawled.

"Matt Drury is at the meeting. It would be best if he didn't see you."

"What else?"

"There must be absolute secrecy about this, as you can see. If Drury ever finds that the Governor has schemed behind his back to make this railroad possible, it will breed trouble."

"And lose a lot of campaign money," Teacher said. "That all?"

"No. Give me an hour and I'll have word of the Governor's amnesty spread around town, so it'll be safe for you to travel the streets. Safer, that is, than it would be now."

Teacher rose, smiling faintly, and the Commissioner did likewise. They faced each other, one a small, smiling man and the other a tall man whose face was flushed with agitation. "Just one more thing, Teacher," the Commissioner said. "There's twelve thousand five hundred dollars deposited in the bank here in your name this afternoon. That's through the Governor's kindness, so that you'll have expense money. But if you skip the Territory with that money, I'll personally see that the whole West is made so hot for you that you'll be glad to hide in the Territorial pen." He paused, then added, "I'm sorry this Territory has fallen on such hard times that it calls on your stripe to help it out."

Sam Teacher's eyes, which had been directed toward the

portrait, flicked over to the Commissioner. He looked at him a long moment, then laughed. His glance returned to the portrait. "I figured it was heavier," he said, and went out, without any good-by.

CHAPTER THREE

SAM TEACHER stood in the doorway that separated the lobby of the Exchange House from its dining room, and by his side stood the clerk.

"He's right over there against the wall, his back to us," the clerk said.

"Who's that with him?"

"His daughter, Celia."

"Okay. Thanks."

"You want to talk to him?"

"I'll wait."

He went back into the lobby, which was almost deserted now, and settled back in one of the deep chairs. In repose, his face lost some of its hardness, and the way his unruly hair was slicked down with water gave him a boyish appearance. He knew it, too, for this was part of the plan. Sitting there, he felt very satisfied. Six one-thousand-dollar bills composed the inner sole of each boot. He was literally walking in money, he reflected.

He stifled the frivolous reflections, however, and considered his plan. It had its disadvantages, of course, the main one being that the role of repentant sinner did not appeal to him. Still, the stakes were high enough to be a temptation. Added to that was one fact that he was shrewd enough to consider. It did not come to every man outside the law that he had one chance to square himself, legally, with the rest of the world. Anyone who passed up such a chance was a fool.

He squirmed in his seat, spat on the floor, and suddenly pulled himself up. He'd have to cut out little things like that, even if they had become part of his nature. He decided to sit there and look like a nice, decent young puncher who respected authority, his pay check, and his boss.

But in five minutes he had both legs over the arm of the chair and was taking practice sights with his six-gun at the knots in the dark paneling of the lobby. The clerk, scowling, came over to him.

"You can't do that here."

"I'm doin' it, ain't I?" Sam asked softly.

"Then you'll have to get out."

Sam swung his feet to the floor and stood up, a thin smile on his face. Something in his expression made the clerk back away. Suddenly Sam thought of his resolve, and looked down at his gun. He sighed deeply and holstered it and said, "Okay, I'll quit."

He managed to sit still, to look like a man waiting for someone, for a full minute until Matthew Drury and his daughter stepped through the dining-room door. With the light of the dining room behind him so that his face was in shadow, Matthew Drury had the look of a middle-aged, tall, and solid rancher, by whom the world has done the best it knows how. His shock of white hair, his thick and bristling eyebrows gave just the touch of fierceness that his benevolent appearance needed. But once face to face with him, you saw that something had happened. Buried between high cheekbones and the thick eyebrows were eyes, brown to blackness, that carried the distillation of arrogance. There was nothing kind or good-humored, nothing tolerant or loving in them. Blindfolded, he would look like a nice old gentleman; without a blindfold he was insolent power incarnate.

Sam, however, was too far away to see that. Besides, he was looking at the girl, who hardly came to Drury's shoulder. There was a sullen, sultry, dark loveliness about her that made Sam swallow involuntarily.

He stood up, yanked off his hat, walked over to them, and said, "Mr. Drury."

Matthew Drury paused and turned and looked down at Sam. He didn't say anything for a moment and then he said, "I know you, don't I?" in a deep, impatient voice.

"Sam Teacher," Sam said.

Drury's eyes narrowed a little. "Oh, yes. They haven't hanged you yet?"

"I'd like to talk with you."

"Well, go ahead."

"Alone, I mean—in private."

"Young man," Drury said, "I have no money in my wallet, my daughter has no jewels with her, there is nothing of value in my room, and I am unarmed. I can't think of anything you'd want with me."

Sam's face flushed a little, and he felt his temper edging him. He also remembered the resolve. He managed a humorless smile and said, "I don't want money, I can't use jewels, I don't want a gun fight. All I want is to talk with you."

Celia Drury was watching him closely. She looked up at her father and said, "Is this Sam Teacher—the outlaw?"

Drury nodded.

"But I thought he was a grown man," Celia said.

Sam looked at her coldly, his blue eyes lighting with venom as she scanned him from head to toe and said, "Talk with him, Dad. You can't mean he's dangerous."

Drury smiled faintly and said, "Come upstairs, Teacher."

By the time they were up the long stairway, Sam had control of his temper. The rooms they entered were the finest that a frontier hotel could provide. The lamps were lighted, and a Spanish maid rose from a chair at their entrance and vanished. Celia sank down into one of the chairs and regarded Sam with frank curiosity. Drury, however, stood in the middle of the room.

"He said in private, Celia."

"I heard him. Still, I want to hear an outlaw talk."

"Leave the room, please," Drury said a little sternly.

"I don't think I will," Celia said. "I want to hear it."

"And I don't want you to!"

They glared at each other a long moment, and then Drury turned to Sam. "You'd better wait until tomorrow when a certain spoiled young lady isn't intruding."

"That's okay," Sam said quietly. "It's about a job."

"A job? With me?"

"That's right."

"Teacher, I don't rustle cattle or steal horses or employ gunmen."

Sam, holding an even grip on his temper, said, "Did you hear about the Governor giving me amnesty?"

Drury inclined his head. "One of his major mistakes," he observed. "I can't imagine why he did it."

Sam flushed but went on: "I'm all square with the law now, Drury. I'd like to start out with a clean slate. Still, there ain't a rancher in the country that'd give me a job. They're afraid of me."

"With good reason."

"All right. Only, I got to live. I'll stay out of trouble just as long as I can feed myself, but what if I can't do that?"

"This sounds like blackmail," Celia Drury observed.

Drury glanced angrily at her and then looked back at Sam. "So you want me to take you on and give you work—keep you out of circulation, so to speak?"

"I never meant it that way."

"Can you punch cattle?"

"No."

"Can you break horses?"

"Anything you got."

"What else can you do? Do you understand breeding, range conditions, moving stock, marketing it, grading it? Do you know anything about ranching?"

"No."

"Then how could I use you?"

"I dunno," Sam said. He was about to add, "You can't," and walk out, when he looked over at Celia and saw the contemptuous smile on her face. He remembered what she had said down in the lobby, and he resolved that he would get even with her if it took him a lifetime.

"Maybe you could teach him to milk cows," Celia said.

Drury paid no attention to her. He stood up and walked over to the window and looked out onto the plaza. "All right," he said, without turning around. "I suppose success imposes obligations on people. And it's true what you said, Teacher. If you can't feed yourself, you'll start preying on us again. I reckon I can afford that protection." He turned to face Sam. "Report as soon as you can to Gates, my foreman. I'll send word up to him tonight."

Sam said, "Thanks," turned and went out. He paused in the hall and took a couple of deep breaths. So this was the way the rich treated you. Like a bothersome hornet, or a red ant. This was what virtue got you, a kick in the teeth. Well, that was all right. He'd known that before he asked for the job. All he had to do was act simple, keep his mouth shut, his eyes open, find out Drury's weakest spot, and strike there. After that he'd make that sharp-tongued little filly sneer on the other side of her mouth.

Suddenly he threw his hat on the floor, picked it up, punched it twice, and went downstairs.

Out on the plaza the saloons were doing their usual booming business with the army men, the legislators, the stockmen, and the punchers from the surrounding country.

Sam headed for the Territorial Bar. His frame of mind was such that he ignored all greetings and made no pretense of being careful. He would have welcomed a fight, amnesty or no amnesty, as his face proclaimed when he shouldered through the batwing doors of the Territorial Bar. It was the grandest saloon in the Territory and had a bar of walnut as dark as old molasses and shiny as the magnificent mirror behind it.

Sam's trouble-seeking gaze roved the bar, but the only acquaintance he recognized was Kate Shore, the owner. She was a fat old harridan of fifty with a face ravaged by time and all the hard passions of her youth. A shrewd gambling head had bought the place, and square games, the best whisky, and a kind of high-toned decorum kept it for her.

At sight of Sam, she tucked the black cigar she held in her hand back in her mouth and moved toward him.

"Hello, son," she said, putting out a leathery hand.

"Hi, Grandma," Sam growled.

"What'll you have?"

"Whisky."

She looked at him shrewdly. "Sure you won't explode it when you get it?"

"I'll wring your neck if I don't," Sam said quietly.

"Okay, okay," Kate said. She put the bottle on the bar and leaned back, watching him pour his drink and down it. Afterward he looked at her, and then a sheepish grin stole over his face.

"Proddy tonight, hunh?" Kate said.

"Plenty."

"Sore because you nicked the Old Man for a full pardon?"

"That was all right," Sam admitted.

"It was lucky," Kate told him. Evidently she considered the trouble was over, for she sidled up to the bar and took the cigar from her mouth.

"Who's around?" Sam asked.

"Nobody you'd be interested in," Kate said idly. "Not till you cool off, anyhow."

Sam looked at her. "I'm cool. Who's around?"

Kate stared at the tip of her cigar. "How do you feel about a little business talk, Sam? Proddy, peaceful, or just *poco-poco?*"

"Poco-poco."

"Enough to talk to a man you don't like much?"

Sam regarded her closely. "Who?"

"Santee Bales."

Kate watched his face slip into a contained hardness.

"Why, I'd be proud to," Sam said. "Where is the Big Wind?"

Kate shook her head. "I can tell that look of yours.

Forget it."

"Where is he?"

"Lookin' the way you do now, you'll never find out from me," Kate said.

Sam laughed. "All right. I ain't mad, Grandma."

Kate only smiled and shook her head.

"He's got a proposition, you say?"

"So he says."

"Ninety for him, ten for me, eh?"

Kate said with extra mildness, "Sam, there's not a boy out of didies in the Territory that hasn't heard about you and Santee. You've fought in every sizable town west of the Pecos. You've thrown one place after another into turmoil, just because you hated each other. You had a gun fight in the Governor's anteroom. Whenever you are both in town, hell pops just like it did today. But have you two ever stopped to think how far you could go if you throwed in together?"

"I ain't," Sam murmured. "Has Santee?"

"Maybe he is right now."

Sam straightened up. "Okay. He can always talk. Where is he?"

Kate put out her hand. "I'll take that gun."

Suspicion crept into Sam's eyes, and Kate laughed. "Do you think I'd sell you out like that, Sam? How long would I live if I did? I've got his gun. Give me yours if you want to see him."

Sam lifted his gun to the bar. "Where is he?"

"In my office. Alone. Go see him."

Sam walked back to the door at the end of the bar and stepped into the room. At the desk, under the kerosene lamp, Santee Bales came to his feet.

His metamorphosis since the afternoon was complete. Freshly shaved, he wore a black broadcloth coat and checkered vest, fancy boots and string tie. The black mustache over his curved wide mouth was twisted a little as he smiled.

Sam leaned back against the door and turned the lock,

looking at Santee. "That was pretty crude this afternoon, Santee."

"It was, wasn't it?" Santee agreed. "Still, I never pass up a chance to get you in a jam."

"Kind of hard on your men, isn't it?"

Santee shrugged, then indicated a chair. "Sit down."

"I'll stand."

Santee sat down in the chair behind the desk, drew a cigar from his pocket and put it in his mouth.

"Well?" Sam said.

Santee lighted the cigar and dropped the match. "I heard you're running with the hounds again," Santee observed. "Every time you get the country in a lynchin' mood, you pull somethin' like this out of the hat."

"Well?"

"What were the conditions of the amnesty, Sam?"

"That I'd give up drinkin' water and stick to whisky. The Governor has an interest in all the distilleries in the Territory."

Santee smiled. "Drury is a hardcase, Sam," he murmured.

Sam's face didn't change. "Drury who?"

"Quit it. You got an amnesty and twenty-five thousand from the Governor if you could get a right-of-way for the Southwestern and Rio Grande through Matt Drury's grant within the next forty days. Right?"

"You're talkin'. I'm just listenin'."

"Because Drury doesn't like the railroad, and because the Governor doesn't want his part in this known, the right-of-way will be signed over to you directly—if you get it."

"Well."

Santee laid his cigar on the edge of the desk and leaned forward, folding his hands. "Suppose, instead of signing the strip over to you, Drury signed it over to say—the Teacher-Bales Land Company, Incorporated." He paused, watching Sam.

"I'm still listening."

"All right. The Territory needs the railroad. It needs it so bad that the Governor is willing to spend twenty-five thousand besides the price of the land to get it. The railroad needs to come in here; they want to tap this territory. Are you still listening?"

Sam nodded, and Santee leaned back in his chair. "They'll want it bad enough, I think, to pay the Teacher-Bales Land Company about a hundred thousand dollars for the right-of-way."

"I double-cross the Governor, in other words."

"What do you owe him?"

"And you, what do you do?"

"I help you get the right-of-way from Drury."

Sam had been leaning against the door. Now he reached in his shirt pocket, pulled out a sack of tobacco dust, and rolled a smoke. He lighted it, inhaled deeply, and strolled over to the desk. Placing both hands on it, he leaned over, looking Bales directly in the eye.

Maybe it was the light of warning in Sam's eyes that told Santee. He put his hands on the arms of his chair, trying to heave himself erect, just as Sam shoved on the desk. Its edge slid over the chair arms, forced Santee down in the chair, and then, pushing the chair and Santee in front of it, moved back against the wall. Santee, his arms under the desk, his back against the wall, was trapped in his seat, helpless as a tied steer.

Sam stood there, watching him in silence. Fear crept into Santee Bales's eyes.

"You can't get away with it, Sam!" Bales said. "I've got men out there! They'll cut down on you!"

Sam said gently, "Squirm, Santee," and smiled.

"This was a truce, Sam. We're not fightin' now. I only wanted to make you the proposition."

Sam laughed now. He climbed up onto the desk and sat down, tailor-fashion, scarcely a foot from Santee. Struggle as he might, Santee could not get a purchase to lift the desk.

Sam looked around him, saw a paperknife and picked

it up, testing its blade with the edge of his thumb. "Pretty dull," he murmured. "Still, a man's ears aren't so tough."

"Listen, Sam . . . you wouldn't do that!"

Sam threw back his head and laughed. Santee, drops of sweat beading his forehead, watched him closely. Suddenly Sam's face was grave.

"Santee," he said, "I don't like you. I'm goin' to kill you some day. But before I do, I want to tell you something." He touched his own chest with bent forefinger. "I gave the Governor my promise, Santee. Maybe you don't know it, but the way I live is by keepin' my promises. I keep 'em, you hear? You want to hear me make one to you, Santee?"

Santee did not answer.

"Here it is. Some day I'm goin' to give you a six-gun and six shells and I'll take a six-gun and six shells, and one of us is goin' to wind up deader than hell. And it's goin' to be you, Santee. That's my promise."

Santee still didn't say anything. Sam looked down at the bottle of ink on the desk, then looked back at Santee. Suddenly he picked up the ink bottle, uncorked it, and dipped his finger in it.

"There ought to be a mark for someone like you, Santee, if I can only think what it is." He paused, scowling. "Let's see. You'd rather double-cross a man than eat a square meal. Maybe that's what it ought to be."

Dipping his finger in the ink again, he drew two crosses on Santee's forehead, two more on his chin, two on each cheek, then leaned back to survey his work. Santee was cursing him with vicious thoroughness. As a final touch, Sam painted his nose black, then corked the ink and climbed off the table.

He touched his hat with a mocking gesture. "So long, Santee."

CHAPTER FOUR

Five days later, at seven o'clock in the morning, Sam Teacher rode into Drury's Star 22 spread and presented himself to Gates, the foreman. The bunkhouse, low and long, and the cookshack adjoining it were of stone, and formed two sides of a rough, sandy plaza. Opposite sides were taken up by the blacksmith shop and the several wagon sheds, while behind them were the barns and the corrals. All this, the working heart of the ranch, sprawled under tall cottonwoods some distance from the house, which was barred from it by a high stone wall.

Sam really didn't see the house that day. He left his horse at the blacksmith shop, inquired for Gates, and was told that he would be at the ranch office, a room off the north end of the bunkhouse. The whole layout gave Sam pause to think. It was like Mexico, where the peons and vaqueros lived off by themselves in a village under the shadow of the proud hacienda. Something about it, the aristocracy of the big house, its aloofness, its wall, was faintly undemocratic and irritating.

Sam stepped up to the door, saw a man at a roll-top desk, his back to the window beside the door, and knocked. Gates—he was called "Pearly," Sam knew—said, "Come in," and did not turn around. Sam stepped in, looking at the bridles, the saddles, the boots, the guns, the old calendars, and the almanacs that were scattered all over the floor and even covered the lone chair.

When he had finished writing, Gates turned around, and Sam saw a man of middle age with a square, kind face and a head of iron-gray, scrub-brush hair. Gates's mustache, like a generous handful of hay plastered on his upper lip, was ragged enough to hide his mouth. The only other giveaway to the man were the wrinkles around his friendly gray eyes.

"I'm Teacher," Sam said.

Gates nodded and said, "I reckoned so. Don't want the job very bad, do you, son?"

"I'm here, ain't I?" Sam said carefully.

"A day late, yes."

"I spent a day in McHarg. Besides, Drury didn't name a date."

"No. Still, you weren't in any hurry." Gates picked up his greasy Stetson and said, "Come along."

They walked out past the sheds, skirted the barn and one corral, and stopped at a second, a large one where a dozen horses were stomping flies. "Ever clean a corral?" Gates asked.

"No."

"You're young enough to learn. Hitch up a team to the small wagon in the shed, load the manure on that, and haul it out to the north pasture beyond the ditch."

Sam looked at the size of the corral with sudden distaste. And then a faint smile creased his face. A man with twelve thousand dollars in his boots shoveling manure for a living! But a promise was a promise. "Okay," he said mildly.

His reply came as something of a surprise to Gates, who had expected him to refuse. Gates said, amused. "You haven't asked about your wages."

"They can't be much," Sam said.

"All right. What about your name?"

Sam's glance shuttled to him. "What about it?"

"What handle do you want to go by?"

"What's the matter with the one I got?"

Gates shifted to his other foot and spat. He was not much taller than Sam, but much more solid, and there was a kind of deliberation in his movements and speech that made Sam trust him.

"Fella," he said slowly, "I'm all for you. I'm all for Drury givin' you a chance. But I ain't the average man. The crew here, like every other crew in the Territory, has talked over your hell-raisin' many a night. Some think you're tough, some don't. But they all aim to find out." He paused. "Get what I mean?"

"Sort of."

"Sam Teacher workin' for puncher's wages is just a laugh. By the time they find it ain't a laugh, somebody's goin' to be dead or hurt. The rest will quit, drift, or sulk. But Jim Melody, say, is just a kid that don't know much except horses. They'll call him a runt, maybe, and he'll get sore and whip a few of 'em into line and they'll like him. See the difference?"

"Jim Melody suits me."

"All right. The harness is in the barn. That pair of grays in the first corral will do." And he turned and walked off.

Sam grinned after him. He was not grinning at Gates, whom he liked instinctively, but at himself. In his boots was twelve thousand dollars—enough to buy a small spread. Yet it had to be earned. It wasn't quite clear to him how shoveling manure into a wagon was going to earn it, but he might find out.

He harnessed the grays, drove them over to the wagon, hitched them up, let down the corral gates, and put the wagon inside. He had a fork and a shovel, and there was the manure, so he got to work, whistling idly to himself and making friends with whatever horses came over to watch him. . . .

Sam heard the man first and looked up to see a slim, weather-tanned young puncher throw his saddle and blanket over the corral fence. The puncher climbed over then, his rope in his hand. Once on the ground, he took a careful look at Sam.

"Who are you?" he asked.

Sam straightened up and looked at him just as carefully. He noticed particularly the sulky face, the flat and rope-muscled shoulders, and the pair of fancy boots.

"Jim Melody," he said, and added in explanation, "new hand."

"Well, drive that team out of here while I snake out a horse."

Sam's eyes narrowed. Was this the first sample of rawhiding that a new hand always got? He reflected a moment and decided that it wasn't. A man couldn't rope a horse that was circling a team and a wagonload of manure. The request was reasonable—only it hadn't been a request. He only nodded, however, and said, "Watch the gate."

The puncher went over and opened the gate and Sam drove out, afterward climbing back on the corral poles to watch. He rolled a cigarette with his small hands, grateful for the intermission.

The puncher singled out a long-legged, blaze-faced chestnut that was as wild as a Hallowe'en night, and made a rope cast. The chestnut, fluid as mercury, dodged it easily, and the remuda started to mill, bunching and then circling.

Sam observed that the puncher was not in a pleasant mood. There are two ways of cursing a horse, one pleasantly, the other meaningly, and the puncher was going at it the meaning way. Sam's attention was sharpened as the puncher made his second cast. By merely looking at the horse Sam knew that this was no game. The horse was afraid, and he was doing his best to escape the rope. The second cast missed, and again the puncher cursed. The third time he shook out his rope and went at it more carefully. He singled out the horse, crowded him, and passed up two chances for a throw. The third time, the chestnut made the mistake of trying to cut back when it was too late.

The rope snaked out, circled his neck, and was drawn taut. The puncher raced for the snubbing post, took a dally, and then watched the horse. The chestnut was fighting with all his might, and the puncher waited until he was choked down. Then he started to walk toward him.

At sight of the approaching man, the horse made a lunge for him, reared, and struck out. The puncher easily dodged, stepped back to the post, and stood there cursing the trembling horse in a voice choked with rage.

Suddenly he took a couple of extra turns around the snubbing post, dropped his rope, and ran for the far side of the corral. Sam watched while he walked up to a length of heavy chain, yanked it down, and started back for the horse.

"Easy, fella," Sam called.

The puncher stopped, glaring at him. "I'm goin' to beat the everlasting hell out of that nag if I break this chain. You stay out of it!"

Sam slipped down off the top pole, dropped his cigarette, pulled up his Levi's, and walked over to the puncher.

"If you want to ride that horse, I'll help you break him."

"Get out of the way!"

"As soon as you put that chain down!"

They were facing each other now, Sam between the horse and the puncher. A good six inches shorter than the puncher and twenty pounds lighter, Sam stood there barring his way.

The puncher studied him carefully. "I've never beat up a kid yet. If you don't move, I'll begin."

"Just drop the chain and you won't have to," Sam drawled.

The puncher raised his hand and slapped Sam across the face. "Move."

Sam reached out and slapped back, harder. "I don't think so."

The puncher dropped his chain, and did not even bother to square off. He took a swing at Sam, who ducked quickly and threw a stiff punch into the taller man's midriff, rocking him back on his heels. The second of surprise on the puncher's face was now washed out by anger. He lunged at Sam, arms flailing.

Sam dodged and weaved, giving ground, until with a

wild swing the puncher was open and off balance. Like a skittering dust-devil, Sam was inside his guard. A right and a left to the head straightened the puncher up, and a smoking uppercut drove him back. Sam followed, throwing in hard, close punches, driving the bigger man back step by step until his back was brought up against the corral poles.

He hunched there, his arms over his face, and Sam dropped his guard, blowing hard. Immediately the puncher exploded at him. A solid right landed on Sam's jaw and he took three steps backward, lost his balance, and sprawled on his back—squarely between the legs of the trembling chestnut.

It was as if the horse somehow understood that this man was fighting for him, for he did not move. Sam scrambled to his feet, his head whirling, and put out a steadying hand on the horse's neck. Still the chestnut did not flinch.

The puncher, mouth and nose bleeding and one eye already purple and swollen, came at him. This time Sam gave ground, covering up, letting the wild blows glance off his arms and his lowered head.

It was when his head was lowered inside his guard that he saw the kick coming. It caught him on the thigh, half turned to avoid it. A red curtain of anger seemed to mount before his eyes as he looked up at the puncher's furious face.

And then, casting caution to the winds, he started in. For a moment they stood toe to toe, slugging wildly, and then Sam, knowing he could not win in this kind of battle, ducked. A wild swing whistled over his head, leaving the other wide open. With all his hard muscled weight, Sam drove a blow at the heart. The man's guard came down with a grunt. Sam waited just that split second he needed to brace himself, and then looped a right and a left to the jaw.

The man sprawled on his back, groaned, rolled over on his side as if to get up, then rolled back and lay there, breathing quietly.

Sam looked up to see Gates and two punchers atop the corral poles. They regarded him with a curious expression until Gates said to the other two, "Well, what are you waiting for?"

They climbed over and approached the prostrate puncher, kneeling beside him. "He's gonna' lose about twelve hours out of his life," one puncher observed, looking over at Gates.

"All right. Carry him out."

The two punchers looked at Sam with a kind of awed amusement. He wrapped a bandanna about his skinned knuckles and leaned back against the fence, dragging in great deep breaths of air.

Gates watched the two punchers carry off their burden and then he turned to Sam.

"Well, son, if you'd thought a week you couldn't have used worse judgment."

"Why?" Sam asked.

"That's Steve Drury, the boss's son."

Sam looked at Gates a long moment and grinned. Gates grinned back and shook his head. "It's tough, all right, but I'll have to give you your time tonight. What was the trouble?"

Sam indicated the chestnut. "He was goin' to comb over that horse with a length of chain." The evidence was there for anyone to see it—the rope still on the horse, the length of chain lying near by on the clean corral floor.

Gates nodded grimly. "Instead of firin' you, I ought to thank you, damn it. A lot of us has wanted to do that for a long time." He looked at Sam with something bordering on affection. "Better go clean up and get some grub before you ride out."

He went with Sam up to the bunkhouse, where Sam stripped off his shirt and bathed his bruises. He wanted to curse the luck that had made him choose the boss's son to fight, but he couldn't. He was glad he'd done it. All his good resolves had amounted to nothing; he had held his job half a day.

At the noon meal, the few punchers who were working around the ranch took him in at once. The fight wasn't mentioned, but Nick Armbruster, the young and burly puncher who had helped carry Steve Drury out of the corral lot, offered Sam his sack of tobacco when the meal was finished.

Sam smoked in silence, listening to the ranch talk. Somehow the ragging, the good-natured swearing, the easy camaraderie of the mess shack made him wish that the fight had never happened. He would have liked this job, he thought.

After dinner, he went into the bunkhouse, picked up his bedroll, and went out to the corral where his buckskin had been turned in. Gates was nowhere around when he whistled his horse over and saddled up.

Leading his horse through the corral gate, he saw Gates coming over to him.

"The boss wants to see you," Gates said.

"Drury?"

"He got in this mornin'."

Sam scrubbed his jaw, looking at Gates. "He may want to see me, but I don't reckon he will."

"Why not?"

"I can get fired without a speech, can't I?"

"Maybe you better do it," Gates suggested.

Sam shrugged, and then a faint grin creased his face. "All right," he said. It might be a pleasure to tell Drury that his son was the kind who would beat a horse with a chain.

He followed Gates through the plaza. Then they stepped through a door in the wall into a large, stone-floored patio. The big house was a two-story stone one, with a gallery on all four sides. It formed one side of the patio, while two single-story adobe wings formed the other two.

Gates headed across the patio toward a room in one of the wings. He knocked on a door and was told to enter;

they both stepped into a large, low-ceilinged room with a floor covered with big Navajo rugs. Its walls held a gun rack, two buckskin ceremonial costumes of some Plains Indians, and a large calendar from a packing house in Omaha. A huge roll-top desk filled one corner, and there were several leather chairs flanking a big fireplace.

Drury was seated in one of the chairs. He said, "Sit down, both of you."

Sam perched warily on the edge of a chair, while Gates leaned against the fireplace. Sam's knuckles were smarting, and one side of his face was aching with a dull throb. He waited for Drury to speak, knowing what he would say, and his own retort was already shaping. He had been humiliated once at Santa Luz by Celia Drury, he had begged for a job, he had shoveled manure, and he had got in a fight. All this because there was a railroad right-of-way in question. And he was farther from getting it than he had been a week ago.

"Teacher, I don't know how to begin this," Drury said.

"Why don't you begin by sayin' you'll have me horse-whipped off the place?" Sam said.

Drury looked at him with those predatory eyes. "Because I don't contemplate doing anything of the kind."

"Arrested, then," Sam amended.

"Nor arrested." Drury pulled himself forward in his chair. "I don't think you understand me very well, Teacher."

"The only chance I got was when your daughter was sharpshootin' there in the hotel room."

Drury flushed. "All right, we're down to cases. Let's start with my daughter. Or better yet, with Steve. She's just like Steve."

"All right, start."

"In the first place, I want to thank you for giving Steve a beating."

"*Por nada.* I wish I could have done better."

"So do I," Drury said grimly. "He's had it coming to him for a long, long time. At least I've got one man working for me who will stand up to a spoiled kid and make him like it." He looked at Gates now, who shifted uncomfortably. "Now what happened out there?"

"What was it over, you mean?" Sam asked.

"Yes."

"What did he say?"

"He said you came up behind him when he was trying to saddle a horse and knocked him down. He was so dizzy after that that he couldn't defend himself."

"He was aimin' to beat a horse with a chain," Sam said quietly.

Drury's face tightened a little. "Then what?"

"I stopped him. He got on the prod and slapped my face. I slapped his and then the fight began. That's all there is to it."

Drury rose and walked to the corner of the room. Then he wheeled and came back and paused before Sam. "What do you think of a man who beats a horse with a chain?"

"Not much."

"What do you think of a girl who owns Chihuahua dogs only so she can make them fight to amuse her?"

"Not much," Sam said again.

"Neither do I," Drury said. He sat down again, this time on the edge of his chair. "I've got a ranch here that I earned," he said quietly. "When I was sixteen, I was a scout in the Mexican War. I made a stake in Virginia City, and cleaned up on the Texas trail drives. I slaved for fifty years to get this ranch, and it's a good one." He paused. "I've raised a son. In twenty-one years he's killed eleven horses and gambled away a fortune. I've raised a daughter who insults the Governor, wears a dress once and throws it away, and gets pleasure out of torturing things, me included." He looked at Sam now. "What's wrong?"

Sam glanced uneasily at Gates, whose face was blank. The idea of Matt Drury, the richest rancher in the Territory, asking advice of Sam Teacher was ridiculous. He had come in here expecting another fight, and to be fired.

Instead he was listening to Matthew Drury unburden his soul.

He took a deep breath and scowled. "The trouble ain't with them, Drury, it's with you."

Drury looked at him and said, "I've suspected that. What can I do?"

"Give that kid a stake, a small stake, and kick him out. If he don't hang, you'll end up proud of him. Take that girl, give her a room the size of a wagon bed, a good dress and a work dress, and make her run the house. No work, no eat."

"But what good is it for a man to work if he can't give things to his children?" Drury asked.

"You ought to know that better than me," Sam said.

"Make 'em or break 'em, eh?"

"They're no good the way they are."

Drury stood up. "All right," he said slowly. He stared at the floor a long moment, then looked at Sam. "Your job from now on is breaking horses at ten dollar a head. Do you want it?"

Sam stared at him. "You mean I ain't fired?"

"Not unless you want to be."

Sam looked over at Gates and got no help, then looked back at Drury. "I don't get it," he said slowly.

Drury laughed briefly, without humor. "It would take you a long time to, Teacher. Pearly over here has raised Steve and Celia from kids. He thinks as much of them as I do—and he can't handle them as well. Every man on the crew around here keeps quiet to save his job. So does the help here in the house. My wife is dead. My friends like me—like me too well to tell me the truth." He shrugged. "So I go to you—a stranger who dislikes me and has got the guts to say he dislikes my kids, too—I go to you for the truth. I get it. I keep you. Does that make sense?"

"Some."

"Then get on with your work."

Outside the door, Sam stopped and turned to Gates. "He drunk?"

Gates chuckled. "Dead sober—for the first time in his life."

Sam shook his head and they started across the patio. Halfway across it, a girl's voice drawled, "Hello, Pearly."

Gates pulled up and looked over at the house. Leaning against a pillar of it, her gray dress silver against her dark skin, was Celia.

"Hello, honey," Gates said, and waved to her. He and Sam started out again.

"Wait a minute," she called.

Sam said to Gates, "I'll off-saddle and throw my bedroll in the bunkhouse," and started for the gate.

"I said wait!" Celia said sharply from behind him.

Sam was almost to the door in the wall, but he stopped and turned slowly, waiting. Celia pushed past Pearly and came up to Sam.

"The help around this place usually come when I call them," she said.

"What of it?"

"I called you."

"I didn't hear you say anything but 'wait.'"

"I meant you."

"Here I am."

She glared at him for a long second, then said, "If you even stay around this country for a day, my father will run you out of it with dogs."

Sam laughed quietly. "Funny way to treat one of his crew."

"But you aren't one of his crew!"

"Ask him."

She whirled and asked Gates, "Is that true, Pearly? Didn't Dad fire him?"

Pearly said no, and Celia said, "You mean after that beating he gave Steve, Dad is still keeping him on?"

"That's right," Pearly said.

She whirled back to Sam, speechless for a moment. The smile on his face touched off her anger. She said, "Well, if Steve can't do it, I can!" and she slapped him. She slapped him four times, twice on each cheek, and hard.

Four red streaks appeared on each cheek. He glanced beyond her then, noting the rose bush behind her and the border of stones that edged the walk to the gate. Then his eyes flicked up to her and he took one slow step toward her. "I guess I'll have to give it to you, too," he murmured.

She stood her ground for a couple of seconds, and then fear crept into her face. "Pearly!" she called, and backed up.

Her heel caught on the stone walk border, she lost her balance, screamed, and sat down in the rose bush. She screamed some more then, putting her hands down gingerly to lift herself up and jerking them away from the thorns. Sam stepped back and laughed quietly. Pearly turned away.

"Get me out of here!" she raged.

Sam walked over to her and put out his hand and she took it. He pulled her up, and before she was even erect she lashed out with her free hand to slap him again.

Sam kept pulling, leaned down, caught her waist with his shoulder, and lifted. When he straightened, Celia Drury was staring at the middle of his back, her head downward.

She beat furiously on his back with her fisted hands, and Sam walked swiftly toward Drury's office. He kicked open the door, walked in, and paused at the first chair. Stopping, he slipped her off into the chair and then turned to face Drury.

"What is this?" Drury asked, his eyes wide.

She made a lunge to get up. Sam put a hand out and pushed her down. "Maybe you better start now, Drury," he said.

Drury's eyes wrinkled a little at the corner. "Maybe I had," he said, as Sam turned and walked out.

CHAPTER FIVE

THE SPANISH WORD *trabajo* means labor. So when the peons of a past day, ignoring all the holy patrons on the calendar of saints, chose to name their town Trabajo it indicated that they felt deeply about the matter. And they should have. Trabajo, the seat of the Ortega grant that was the nucleus of Matt Drury's Star 22 holdings, was literally carved out of a cliffside, with the Rio Arriba running its course below. Legend had it that when Don Diego, the original Ortega grantee, was asked why he had worked two hundred peons seven years in constructing the town when he could have moved a mile in any direction and built it on the broad grama grass plains, he had answered, "I am their *patron*. Their sons, and their sons' sons, will live here. Let them remember that it was hard for their forefathers, and they will be content with what little they have."

Save for the fact that it rested on rock leveled by many hands, Trabajo was no different from other towns. The usual plaza held the usual big trees, and false-front and adobe stores flanked all sides of it. There was only one thing about it not apparent to the eye. It was wholly dependent upon Matt Drury's beneficence, just as it had once been dependent upon Don Diego's.

Santee Bales had learned that, just as he had learned that Matt Drury had a beautiful, spoiled daughter, a wastral son, a crew of twenty-odd men, a seventeen-room house, and a well-padded bank account. Of all these, Santee figured that the son was the most accessible and vulnerable, and he had laid his plans accordingly.

Already, through a two-day acquaintance with Charlie, the bartender at the Chamisa saloon on the plaza, he had established the fact that he was a cattle and horse buyer. He had even taken Charlie's advice on two deals that had netted him seven horses he neither needed nor wanted. He had taken a dozen "trips" to establish the fact that he was a busy man. But he was always at the Chamisa around three o'clock, for that was the hour when Steve Drury usually came in, if he came at all.

He was leaning against the forward end of the bar reading the *Territorial News* when he heard the batwing doors swing open. He glanced up at the bar mirror and saw a lean, angry-looking puncher enter. He looked carefully; this puncher had just been in a fight. He had a black eye, several bruises on his face, and his lips were swollen thickly. Santee heard Charlie's respectful: "Hello, Drury," and knew that this was the end of waiting. He merely glanced back at his paper, however, while Drury ordered whisky in a surly tone of voice.

Presently Santee finished his drink and strolled idly over toward the doors, looking out over them. Suddenly he whistled in exclamation and went out. In a moment he came into the saloon again and walked over to Charlie, who was reading the paper Santee had just left.

"Who owns that black out there?" Santee asked in a loud voice.

"I dunno," Charlie said. "What black?"

"I'd like to make a trade with whoever owns him," Santee said. "That's a horse."

"It's mine," Drury said. "He's not for sale or trade."

Santee, needing only this chance, walked over to Drury and praised the horse. In the conversation he managed to state his name, his business, and to buy Drury a drink. The younger man, self-conscious because of his black eye, listened surlily and answered in monosyllables.

It was while Santee was chatting idly that he felt a touch on his elbow and turned to confront an unshaven puncher of middle years. The puncher was a lean, tall, bleach-eyed man in clean Levi's, and his speech immediately identified him as a Texan.

"If I'm speakin' out of line, gentlemen, why, say so," he drawled amiably. "Me and my partner has been tryin' to buy into a decent poker game all mornin', but we can't make it more than three-handed. Like a little sport?"

Santee looked at Drury and then said casually, "I'd like a few hands myself. Can't speak for this gentleman."

"Suits me," Drury said promptly.

They moved over to the table where the house man and the Texan's partner were sitting, and the Texan introduced them. His companion was slighter, older, and a suspicious-looking man. None of them seemed to notice the marks of a fight on young Steve Drury, and this served to restore his spirits.

At the start he won. He was a reckless player to begin with and now he played heady, intuitive poker. Santee, his head settled on his thick shoulders, lost for a while and then started to win. The two punchers and the house man lost all the way, and by suppertime Drury was losing a little. When they took time off to eat, it was Drury who suggested that they raise the limit, and the two punchers agreed. Back in the saloon, the evening session set in with a group of quiet idlers watching the game and drinking and gambling at the other tables.

Santee, once the stakes were raised, started winning steadily. The slight puncher, who had lost all the way, was getting surly now, and several times he and Drury were at the point of words.

Drury bet and lost his last chips. He turned to Santee and said, "What's that black of mine worth?"

"Four hundred," Santee said; it was a generous figure.

Drury nodded and kept playing, and kept losing, and the slight puncher kept getting more belligerent. The blowoff didn't come until late in the evening, however. Steve Drury put down a full house, three aces and a pair of fives, to claim a big pot. Santee threw down his hand. The tall puncher swore and threw in his hand. But the slight puncher only looked at Drury's cards, then rose. Without a word, he spread out his hand. He had a full house, too, three sevens and a pair of aces.

"I been wonderin' when I'd catch you, fella," he said slowly to Steve. "I don't mind a five-ace deck, but I hate to get it throwed up to me in a full house."

His hand dived for his gun. Drury lunged away and Santee, who started moving the moment the last word was out of the puncher's mouth, lunged across the table. He grabbed the man's wrist just as his body hit him, and both of them went down over the back of the chair, and then he drove a fist into the other's belly. The puncher gasped, tried to get up, and Santee knocked him down again. Then Santee rose to his feet, picked the puncher up, and knocked him over the table, upsetting it and scattering the chips. The puncher didn't move from the floor.

When Santee looked up, young Drury had the other puncher covered with his gun.

"Pick up that saddle-tramp and get out of here before you both get your necks stretched," Santee said to the Texan.

The Texan, without a word, dragged his partner out the saloon door, and soon they heard them ride off.

Drury, his face a little pale, looked over at Santee.

"That was pretty close," he said.

"A couple of tinhorns," Santee sneered. "They had it framed before we ever started playin'."

Young Drury wiped his face with his bandanna, still looking at Santee. "He'd have shot me."

Santee laughed and said, "Let's have a drink."

At the bar, when the room was quieted, Drury said, "I owe you money."

"That's right."

"How much?"

"That horse and five hundred dollars, I make it."

Young Drury scowled at his drink. "I can't pay you now."

"That's all right with me," Santee said. "The word of Matt Drury's son is good enough for me."

Drury looked uncomfortable. "I dunno, Bales. I'm in trouble with my old man."

"It'll wash out."

Drury shook his head. "He may pay this gamblin' debt for me. I dunno. If he does, it's the last one he'll ever pay. He kicked me out this afternoon. Said he'd give me a small stake and that's all."

Santee looked sympathetic, but Drury evidently did not want to talk about it. Santee took another tack. "Well, in that case, you were a fool for gambling."

"I was."

"Own any horses? I'm a horse trader."

"I've got a big string," Drury said reluctantly. He felt Santee looking sharply at him. "What's the matter?"

"You're kicked out of your dad's house and you own a string of horses. Are they as good horses as that black?"

"Better. He's only fair."

Santee laughed quietly, looking at his drink.

"What's the matter?" Drury asked.

"Ever been in business, Drury?"

"No. Why?"

"You could go into business right now."

"How?"

"You've got a string. The Utes back of your ranch are full of wild horses."

"What of it?"

"Why, all you need to catch wild horses is a string of broke ones to ride 'em down with."

"You mean I ought to start catchin' and breakin' horses for a livin'?"

"Why not?"

"It's hard work," Drury said slowly.

"Sure, but you won't do it. Look here." Santee called for drinks, and when they came he said, "I've got an investment in you, a gamblin' debt, haven't I? You want to pay it back?"

"I never welshed yet," Drury said quickly.

"All right. Then suppose we go in partnership. I put up the money for wages for a dozen men. You put up their mounts as your share. I'm a horse trader so I can sell everything the crew breaks out for us. Don't that make sense?"

Drury's face changed a little, and he smiled through his swollen lips. Suddenly the smile faded. "That's fine," he said, "only we need a place."

"Didn't you say your old man promised you a small stake?"

"That's right."

"Then he'd be pleased if you asked for a piece of land instead of money. Lord knows he's got enough land to spare."

"Sure," Drury said. "Sure. He'd do that."

Santee said carefully, "Of course, you'd have the right to choose what land you wanted. You'd want it as far from him as you could get it. You'd also want it on water. And I'd pick up a place back in the canyon country where you'd be close to where the stuff runs."

"There's plenty of places like that."

"Good," Santee said. "Finish your drink and we'll hunt up a lawyer. You and me will be partners."

Drury laughed with pleasure. "That's quite a favor, Mr. Bales."

"Santee to you, Steve, and it's not a favor. I've got money sunk in you and I'm going to get it out. Fifty-fifty proposition. When I've taken the debt out of the profit I'll sell out to you or stick with you, whichever you want."

By midnight that night, Santee was in possession of a legal document stating that he and Steve Drury were partners. The most important clause in the document, however, was one that young Drury had not even bothered to question. It provided that in case of the death of either partner, the whole property was to revert to the survivor.

Santee said good-by to Drury at the Chamisa, and then headed back toward the hotel. Somewhere along the darkened store fronts, he saw two figures in the shadows and walked up to them.

"Everything all right, Santee?" a man asked. It was the man with a Texas drawl. The other man, the one Santee had hit, was with him.

"Fine," Santee said. "Fine."

"How did it look to you?"

"Convinced everybody in the saloon," Santee said.

"Boss, you sure got a left there that kicks like a mule."

Santee laughed. "It's worth twenty-five dollars, isn't it, Shorty?"

"Fifty," Shorty said.

Again Santee laughed. "All right. Fifty it is. Now fade out of town, you two, and I'll see you in a couple of days."

They left him, and Santee strolled on to the hotel. The thing had worked out perfectly. Young Drury was a fool, unsuspecting and gullible and just selfish enough so that he could be stubborn with his father. By careful handling he could convince young Drury that Rio Medio canyon was the ideal spot for their horse ranch. If young Drury could convince the elder Drury that he should be given it, then Santee Bales had nothing more to worry about. The canyon of the Rio Medio, starting in the high Utes, blanketed the pass that the Southwestern and Rio Grande wanted, and could not get.

CHAPTER SIX

WHEN CELIA DRURY had pulled the bell rope five times without getting an answer from Tonita, her maid, she stormed down the wide stairway to the ground floor, calling, "Tonita! Tonita!"

She found the maid in the kitchen, hiding behind the ample skirts of the cook.

"Didn't you hear that bell, Tonita?" Celia demanded.

"Yes, Miss Celia," the frightened girl answered.

"Then why didn't you come?"

"Mr. Drury, he said I couldn't."

"Couldn't? Couldn't come to me?"

"Yes, miss. I work in the kitchen now, he said."

Celia's eyes narrowed. For the first time in her life she thought it seemly to be dignified before the servants, even if it did stem from a selfish pride. She smiled weakly and said, "That's right. I'd forgotten."

Out in the large dining room, she paused to get control of herself. Now was no time for anger, or for losing her temper. She was fighting something that anger would not help. Her face settled and she went back to the hall. Her father was waiting for her at the foot of the stairs.

"I heard the bell ringing," he said. "Something you wanted?"

"No. I'd forgotten Tonita was working in the kitchen now," Celia answered coldly. She avoided looking at her father.

"What did you want her for?"

"To pack my trunks. I'm going to the Barkers."

Drury's face was stern, but as she said this he suppressed a smile. "I don't think you'll need trunks," he said.

"I'm moving over there for good," she answered quietly.

"That's all right with me. Only you won't need trunks. You'll have one good dress and two work dresses and two pairs of shoes. You can pack all those in a valise."

The color mounted in Celia's face, but something in the set of her father's jaw told her a scene would be useless. She shrugged carelessly. "I don't care much. I have more ordered."

"That you haven't," Drury said quietly. "I've written to St. Louis telling them to refuse you credit."

"They still take money, don't they?"

"Not yours. You don't have any. I've stopped your account at the bank."

There was a moment of utter silence. Celia still had a firm grasp on her temper, although it was shock that made it possible. She gave him a false smile and said, "You do love your children, don't you, Dad?"

"Hardly ever," Drury answered quietly.

"I suppose I'm to walk to the Barkers'."

"No, I'll have a man take you. He's waiting now. But there's something I don't think you wholly understand about future visiting."

"That I'm not wanted?"

"Exactly. The time when you could descend on people with six trunks, a maid, and a crate of dogs is gone. You have nothing to give them now, and I don't think they'll want you to stay long." He paused. "I doubt if they ever liked you well enough to want you to stay long, anyway."

That hurt, and Celia's eyes showed it. But she still did not intend to show any signs of weakness. "At any rate, I won't bother you from now on."

"Not for a week, anyway," Drury answered. "By that time, unless you're pretty thick-skinned, you'll observe that the Barkers have had enough of you. And since you haven't any place else to go, you'd better come back here."

"And work for you, like a kitchen wench?"

"A kitchen wench, yes," Drury said slowly. "Like your mother—or my mother."

He wheeled and started for the door. Suddenly he paused and turned and looked at his daughter. "Haven't we had about enough of this?" he asked in a kindly voice.

Celia said, "When you're through treating me like a dog, I'll come back. And not until then."

Drury smiled, a bit sadly, and went out. Celia climbed the stairs to her room, where Steve was sitting on the bed. When she saw him she closed the door behind her.

"It looks like he means it," Celia said, slowly walking into the center of the room, her face thoughtful.

"I could have told you that," Steve said. "He's on the prod."

"But why? Why? What have I done?"

"It wasn't you," Steve murmured. "It was me and that damn chestnut—and that cocky new hand."

"That little outlaw," Celia said in a low, passionate voice. "Everything was all right until he came!"

"It's still all right," Steve said tightly. "I'll make out with my horse ranch."

"Did Dad give you any land?"

"Told me to take my choice and he'd give me a deed."

Celia sighed. "I wish I were a man."

"We'll get even with him," Steve said. He smiled faintly. "Why, I'll break out a bunch of horses that'll be so good he can't afford not to use 'em. And then I'll stick him for them until he yells for help."

Celia looked shrewdly at him. "Steve, you're a simple kind of fool."

Steve looked up at her, surprised. "Why?"

"Nothing's going to make Dad buy your horses. They're wild horses, the same kind we catch and break out here. And if you charged him more than he thought they were worth, he'd laugh at you."

Steve stood up, an injured expression pouting his swollen lips. "You're a lot of help!"

Celia shook her head slowly. "Not much. Only I've got

sense enough to understand that he has us where he wants us. He can do without us a lot better than we can do without him."

Steve laughed shortly. "We'll see about that," he said, and went out. Celia watched the door slam behind him and shook her head, puzzled. Then she set to work. Remembering that there was a large trunk in her closet, she went over to it and opened the door. Where a row of dresses some twelve feet long had hung there were now only three garments. Two pairs of shoes were on the floor beneath them. She stared at them a long moment, and slowly it came to her that her father knew her so well he had anticipated her next move. He had made it impossible to disobey his order.

Grimly she packed the three dresses and two pairs of shoes in the valise and went downstairs with it and out into the patio. She had no intention of saying good-by to her father, although she never intended seeing him again. Drury, from a window in his office, watched her step through the door in the wall. He felt a little sad and a little sorry for what he had done, but he was a stubborn man. He went back to his accounts.

Outside the wall, a buckboard was waiting. Sam Teacher was lounging against a tree talking to Pearly.

Ignoring Sam, Celia said, "All right, Pearly. I'm ready."

Sam walked over to the buckboard. Celia looked at him and said, "There's one consolation about leaving this place. I won't have to look at you."

"The feelin's mutual," Sam replied.

He picked up the reins, ready to climb in. "You're not taking me!" Celia said quickly, looking at Pearly.

Pearly shifted his feet and nodded.

"I won't go!" Celia said, stepping away from the buckboard.

"Matt's orders," Pearly said gently. "This here's the only man I can spare."

"But can't you drive me yourself?"

"I'm goin' over the books with your dad," Pearly said.

Celia looked at Sam. "I suppose this is a little idea of your own?"

Sam shook his head gravely. "No, ma'am. I offered to clean corrals all day to get out of it."

Celia's face colored. Sam climbed into the buckboard, sat down, and looked at her. "The sooner we get it over with, the better we'll both like it," he drawled, adding, "There ain't any back on this seat. You can face backward and I'll face forward."

Under his mustache, Pearly grinned. He came over and hoisted the valise into the buckboard and waited to assist Celia.

"I'd like a saddle horse," Celia said abruptly.

"Good," Sam said, putting the reins down.

"All right," Pearly said.

"No, I don't, either," Celia flared. "I won't be bluffed out by any swaggering little bully like you!" She climbed swiftly onto the seat and sat down. "Good-by, Pearly," she said. "Come and see me."

Pearly waved, and Sam clucked the team into motion. They drove out under the cottonwoods toward the east, the dusty road ribboning out before them.

A ground breeze, swelling up from the south, swayed the grama grass and sent tiny dust-devils skittering across the road. Sam resolved that nothing would induce him to talk to her, but when, after a ten-minute silence, she said, "I think you're behind all this," he forgot his intentions.

He turned to look at her, and found that she was watching him with carefully hostile eyes. "That's likely, ain't it?" he said.

"If it's any satisfaction to you, I've left home."

"It's some," Sam admitted.

"And Steve has, too."

"Well, well."

"Furthermore," she added, her voice rising, "he's going to make a success."

"Of what? Beatin' horses?"

"Breaking them!"

Sam nodded gravely.

"He's starting a horse ranch with a man in town. His partner puts up the capital and Steve supplies the mounts."

"Who puts up the work?"

"They hire it," Celia said coldly. "Dad's giving them a strip of land for the ranch."

"This partner a stranger?"

"Yes, why?"

"Nobody that knew your brother would throw in with him in any business—short of a slaughterhouse."

She didn't speak for a moment, and then she said in a tight, passionate voice, "You're the most insulting man I ever knew!"

"I'm learnin' fast," Sam conceded. "If I could enjoy your company for another week, I'd be mighty good at it."

Celia's surprise overcame her anger. "I? Insulting?"

"Some," Sam said. He took a deep breath and began: "Besides that, you're dead wrong. The only folks that have a right to demand things like you do is a queen—and you ain't a queen. A queen is a lady, or so I've heard my mother say. She's generous and kind and folks can't help lovin' her. You don't qualify. You're selfish and you're mean." He shook his head. "I've been wantin' to get that off my chest before I saw you for the last time. Now we can talk about somethin' else."

Celia Drury didn't answer. The last two hours had not been pleasant ones for her. It wasn't so much that she had been forbidden things she wanted; it was that she couldn't help seeing that people were speaking the truth about her. Her father had hurt her there at the house. And now this Sam Teacher had hurt her again. She was sensible enough to know that it was partly her vanity that was hurt, but it went beyond that. Something was wrong with her. When all the props were pulled out from under her, and she was just an ordinary girl with ordinary clothes and ordinary possessions, she seemed to herself to be something of a shallow braggart, a shrew, and a thoroughly unlikable person.

But where another girl might have wept, she did not. Sam thought it was because she cared so little for anyone's opinion that nothing could touch her, and he was mainly right. But the seed had been planted, the seed of doubt in herself, and she was silent.

The Barkers lived in Trabajo in a large frame house behind the plaza. Sam pulled up at the gate and held the reins while Celia climbed out. He handed her the valise, and she took it without thanking him.

"Some day," she said quietly, looking him straight in the eye, "there's going to be trouble between us. It won't be name-calling trouble, either."

"Some day," Sam drawled, "you're goin' to meet a man you want to marry, and you'll do it. But he'll carry a wagon spoke around with him, and every time you open your mouth, he'll take a swipe at you. He'll beat you and drag you around by the hair, and every time you get in a temper he'll toss you in the horse trough." A slow smile spread over his face. "You'd be pretty nice to know, after he gets through with you. But if you don't meet him, you'll probably get so mad sometime you'll swell up and bust. And when they pick you up, they'll find you're about as big as a handkerchief. The rest of you was just wind."

Celia threw her valise at him. He dodged it easily and drove off, leaving her standing speechless by the road, her valise making a little mound in the dust of the street.

Sam had three errands to do for Pearly, and after finishing them he put the buckboard in at the tie rail before the Chamisa saloon and went inside.

Charlie, who had been looking out the window, came away as Sam entered and bellied up to the bar.

"Ain't them Star Twenty-Two horses?" Charlie asked idly, as he took Sam's order and served the drink. Sam said they were and Charlie asked him if he was a new hand and Sam said he was and they shook hands.

Charlie leaned against the back bar then and lazily

picked his teeth. "Well, looks like the young kid has finally set hisself up in business, don't it?" he observed.

"Looks that way."

"He'll make a go of it, all right," Charlie said.

Sam smiled faintly. "He never even made a go of a poker game, where his chances was fifty per cent better than in anything else."

"Oh, it ain't him," Charlie said. "Hell, he don't count. It's the man he's throwed in with. Knows what he's doin' and how to do it, I reckon."

"He better," Sam said. He put a half dollar on the counter, ready to go.

"Yeah, Bales'll pull him through," Charlie said. "So long, Melody."

Sam, half turned, stopped and turned back to the bar. "Who'll pull him through?"

"Bales. Santee Bales. That's his partner's name."

Sam nodded and strolled out the door. He got into the buckboard, backed out, swung around, and put in at the feed stable up the street.

"I want a horse and saddle," he told the hostler, "and be damn quick about it. A good horse, a stayer."

While the hostler was getting it, Sam thought back over what he had heard from Celia, and piecing all the information together it pointed to just one thing. Santee Bales had in some way talked young Drury into going partners on a horse ranch, Old Man Drury to furnish the land. And, unless Santee was losing his persuasive powers, that land would be the canyon of the Rio Medio, the pass the railroad wanted.

CHAPTER SEVEN

SAM RODE NORTH AND EAST, following the directions the hostler had given him. As he rode across this upland country, rolling and thick with grama grass, he studied the country to the north. The land tilted here in a gradual slope lifting into the foothills of the Utes. Behind them, the mountains towered in a ragged blue range from horizon to horizon, their slopes green with pines. In several places, he noticed, the peaks sloped down to low notches, and any of these would make a pass for the railroad line. He didn't wholly understand the importance of this one canyon, but reserved judgment. After all, the Commissioner should know whereof he spoke.

By midafternoon, however, it became clear. The foothills, whose base seemed to be a fawn-colored plateau, gradually dissolved into separate parts as he approached. And then the reason for the choice of Rio Medio canyon became clear. From a distance, looking toward the mountains, it seemed as if the land tilted gently up to the foothills. It did not. It sloped down. Several miles from the foothills the rolling prairie ceased at the base of a great high fawn-colored rim that blended in with the prairie. It lifted several hundred feet to the flats above, and its face, as far as the eye reached, was unbroken. It was a great wall, and from under it the whole north and the mountains were blotted out. It was a massive barrier of rock.

Sam traveled its face for three hours, heading east, until, rounding a shoulder, a green valley appeared ahead and a little below him.

Pausing, he regarded this spot, his glance following the

valley up to where it knifed through the high rim. The Rio Medio—more a wide stream than a river—fed by springs up in the mountains for centuries, had worn a gently sloping valley through the rim. For fifty miles to either side of it, there was no other gradual descent from this rim. It was here in this canyon the railroad had to lay its tracks for the descent to the plain. And it was here, Sam knew, that Santee Bales would locate his horse ranch.

Sam sloped down into the green valley, keeping to the coulees and to the brush, his glance on the ground for tracks. All he wanted was evidence that he could lay before Matthew Drury. Pearly had told him this morning that Steve was out looking for a location, and chances were that they were in this valley today.

He worked his way closer and closer to the canyon mouth, casting about for any sign of horse tracks. But they were unaccountably missing. Had Santee, to make his choice appear more reasonable, agreed to look at other locations first? Sam halted almost at the mouth of the canyon and debated entering.

Finally he pushed on. Tall piñons and scrub cedar screened the shoulder of rock where the canyon cut into the rim wall. Great boulders broken off in some distant day had slid down to the canyon floor, and they stood like a massive forest through which he threaded his way.

He was looking ahead, his sight alert and carefully searching out this boulder field, or he probably would not have been caught napping. When he did hear the faint hiss above and behind him, he rolled out of the saddle, his hand streaking to his gun. But it was too late, and he felt the rope slap around him, settle to his elbows, and pin them before he was yanked roughly off the horse. He landed on the ground with a breath-jarring thud, tried to roll, was yanked to his knees and then to his face, where he kicked frantically to free himself.

He heard a soft chuckle above him and felt his gun being slid out of its holster. Then the pressure on the rope slackened and he rose to step out of the loop and face a long, bleach-eyed puncher who had a gun pointing at his chest.

"Hello, Tex," Sam said. It was Santee Bales's understrapper and an old acquaintance, one of the two men who had engaged young Drury and Bales in the poker game. Sam turned his head to look at the man who had made the cast. He was standing against a shoulder of rock, coiling his rope.

"Well, well," Sam said. "The lobo twins, Tex and Shorty." He switched his glance back to the Texan. "Why the reception?"

"You wouldn't know, would you?" the Texan drawled.

"I know one thing," Sam murmured. "Let that gun off and you'll have the Governor swarmin' all over you."

"If we wanted to beef you, we wouldn't of roped you, Sammy boy," Tex said. "No, your carcass has to be handled pretty careful."

"What does Santee want of me?"

"Maybe we better go see," Tex said. He gestured to Shorty. "Come here and cover him." He waited until Shorty had flipped his gun out and pointed it at Sam, and then Tex holstered his own. His next move was to hit Sam in the face as hard as he could. Sam saw it coming, almost ducked, but not quite.

It was like a sledge hitting him in the cheek. He sprawled on his back, rolled once, and was brought up against a boulder. Slowly he rose to his feet, dusting his trousers off.

"That was for Runt," Tex said. "Besides that, it was for me, too. I've always wanted to slug that baby face of yours."

Sam's eyes were hard as his glance rose to Tex's and held it. "I never held anything special against you, Tex. But from this second on—"

"Get on that horse," Tex said, smiling with pleasure. Sam mounted, and with Shorty still holding the gun, Tex tied Sam's feet under the horse's belly.

Tex and Shorty mounted, Tex taking the reins of Sam's

horse. They crossed the canyon, heading east, and clung to the base of the rim for two miles. At the mouth of a small *rincon,* a wind erosion in the soft rubble of the talus, Tex turned in. There was enough room to hide a half dozen horses besides a camp. Three pairs of blankets lay around the dead ashes of a fire. A small piñon grew against the rim wall. Sam was ordered off the horse and told to sit down tailor-fashion with his back against the tree. His hands were tied behind the tree, and a loop put about his waist.

Sam said, "Where's Santee?"

"You got a long wait," Shorty said. "Better get some sleep."

Tex rolled into the blankets and dozed off while Shorty kept watch. Sam tried to pry information out of Shorty, but Shorty wasn't talking. The sun set, and Shorty built up a fire. Tex woke up and they cooked a meal and ate it, not bothering to offer Sam any. After that Shorty rolled into the blankets, and Tex settled down to the long night vigil. Occasionally he would look over at Sam and laugh.

"What's funny?" Sam asked finally.

"I won't spoil it for you," Tex said.

Around midnight, Tex rose and walked to the mouth of the *rincon* to listen. Suddenly he dodged back and doused water on the fire.

Sam opened his mouth and yelled, "Help! Help!"

Tex, drawing his gun, cursed him with savage violence, and Sam kept on yelling. Suddenly a booming laugh came across the night and Sam stopped yelling. It was Santee Bales's laugh.

Tex built up the fire, and Santee rode into the *rincon* and dismounted. He looked at Sam and grinned. "Sam Teacher yellin' for help." He shook his head in mock gravity. "What's this country comin' to, Tex?"

Sam said, "Don't I see some ink marks on your face, Santee?"

Santee lunged at him and hit him twice with the palm of his hand. "One more crack like that, Sam, and I'm liable to lose my business head," he said thickly.

"How'd you get it off?" Sam jibed. "Or is that a new face—your other one?"

Santee rose slowly, glaring at him, his hands clenching and unclenching. Then he threw back his head and laughing walked over to the fire. He drank a pot of coffee, ate some jerky and pan bread, and then rolled a smoke. When he was finished, he stepped over to Sam, wiping his hands on his black trousers.

"I want my hands to be clean, Sam," he said, reaching into his inside coat pocket. "I've got a couple of papers here that you'd like to see."

"I know what they are," Sam said shortly.

"Why, bless your heart, of course you do. Only you wouldn't deny me the pleasure of showin' them to you, would you, Sam?"

The first paper he unfolded was the partnership agreement between himself and Steve Drury. The second, the one that Sam didn't like to look at, was the deed to the land.

It simply stated that for purposes of starting a horse ranch, Matthew Drury deeded a strip three miles wide and twenty miles long to his son, Steve Drury. The strip was to be taken from the eastern boundary of the Ortega grant, its longest side running from south to north.

"Know where the east boundary of the Ortega grant is, Sam?" Santee asked softly. "It's old-fashioned, but you ought to understand it. The old title reads that the east boundary of the grant shall be three hundred varas at all points east of the river known as the Rio Medio. Do you know what a vara is, Sam?"

"A yard."

"That's right. Three hundred yards east of every twist and turn of the Rio Medio is the east boundary of my ranch. The west boundary is far enough away so it blankets the canyon. The canyon is seven miles long and my deed says twenty. It's sewed up pretty tight, ain't it, Sam?"

"Tight as you'd want it," Sam agreed.

Santee laughed. "It's even recorded, Sam."

"All right."

Santee pocketed both papers and rolled himself a smoke. Sam could see that Santee wanted to make this moment last as long as he could. He squatted on his haunches now and blew smoke in Sam's face.

"The Teacher-Bales Land Co., Sam. Remember?"

"Yeah."

"How much will the Governor give me, Sam?"

Sam said nothing.

"A quarter million? A hundred thousand? Who knows? And ain't it nice, Sam, that I don't have to split it with a partner?" Again he laughed, and shook his head reminiscently. "I thought you had brains, Sam."

"I have."

"But not enough to join up with me. Not enough to wonder, when you found out young Drury had a partner, why I didn't bother to change my name. Not enough to know damn well what piece of land I was after, and go tell Drury. No, you had to follow me, walk right into Tex's hands." He shook his head and rose. "Maybe I'm the one that didn't have any brains, asking you to join up with me."

He walked over to the fire and poured himself a cup of coffee. He put the cup to his mouth and took it away and spat. Then he took the cup, walked over to Sam, and threw the contents in his face. Tex and Shorty, laughing, followed suit.

"Well, I'll be goin', Sam," Santee drawled. "To Santa Luz. Want me to tell the Governor anything?"

Sam could not open his eyes. He shook his head helplessly. The coffee grounds felt like gravel under his lids.

Santee roared with laughter. "*Adios, amigo.* Think you can get loose?"

"If I ever do, you'll be dead, Santee."

"I heard that before, I remember. Well, the invitation is always open, Sam. *Adios.*"

Sam heard them ride off, but he could not see them, for

he could not open his eyes. He listened a long time to night silences, and finally decided that they had taken his horse, too.

He sat motionless a long while, reflecting on what Santee had told him. It didn't take long to come to the conclusion that Santee had him over a barrel. Where Santee had come in with the old daredevil recklessness of a man who scorns the law, Sam had come into the country like a docile lamb. Why hadn't he done what Santee did—get the deed any way he could and to hell with the law? The Governor would have forgiven any irregularities. But no, he had muffed it from the start, afraid that he might lose that precious amnesty.

From now on, though, he was free of that amnesty. There was just one thing he wanted to do, and he wanted to do it so badly his whole body trembled. That was to face Santee Bales with a gun in his hand.

As soon as he calmed down, he worked patiently at his bonds, and inside of ten minutes his wrists were bleeding. He steeled himself against the pain and worked on, hour after hour. He had to loosen each strand of a lariat, a rope that has to be stretched before it can even be used. By dawn he was able to move his wrists and by daylight he had dragged one bloody hand free. His first act with that free hand was to wipe his eyes of coffee grounds. They smarted like fire, and hurt far more than his wrists.

A can of water had been left by Santee, and when he was free Sam bathed his eyes with it. By full sunup he had them cleaned out, and he took stock of his resources. He was perhaps fifteen miles from Trabapo, on foot, hungry, and without any food or any water. His first move was to get some water. His gun was missing, and after a careful search of the *rincon* for it, he gave it up, then, carrying the lariat which had bound him, he set out for the Rio Medio two miles to the west.

Once there, he drank his belly full to stave off hunger, washed, smoked, and contemplated the walk to town. In high-heeled boots it would take him a day, and he would be a cripple for two days afterward. He resolved to get a horse. Picking up the lariat, he set out.

Following the stream toward the south where it opened onto the plains, he spotted a couple of bands of grazing horses. They would spook at sight of him, he knew, so the best plan was to wait for them to come to water.

He lay in the willows of the stream bank all morning, watching them. When the heat of midday became uncomfortable, the horses started to drift to shade and water. Like an Indian, Sam first tested the wind, then gauged the place where they would hit the stream and set out for it. It was a regular watering place, he found. There was a ford here for a wagon road almost overgrown with grass. The brush had been cleared out on either side of the ford, but a second growth thicker than the first had sprung up. Sam cached himself in this on the downwind side of the ford and waited, his loop built.

There were eight horses in the band, all branded. Sam picked out a bay mare, old and tractable-looking, and waited for her to approach. She sniffed the water, then ambled in, the others following her but considerably less trusting. They kept looking up at the horizon and snorting.

Sam waited until the bay mare had raised her head and looked upwind. Then he stole out of the brush dragging his rope. A blaze-face sorrel saw him and gave a whistle that started the stampede. Even as the mare wheeled in a curtain of water, lunging for the bank, Sam made his cast. It settled around her neck, and immediately she started for the other bank. Sam was dragged through the creek, where he tripped and went under. But he clung to the rope like grim death, came to his feet on the bank, and then dug in his heels. As soon as the mare saw him, she stopped fighting.

Sam worked toward her hand over hand, and when he touched her she trembled a little. He talked to her for several minutes, all the while shaping a hackamore, which he slipped over her head. Then he got ready to mount. He grabbed her mane and swung on. Before he was on her back, she came uncocked and threw him over her head. He held the rope end, however, and came back to her.

He went through the same soothing talk again. The second time she did the same thing, only this time he had found his seat. Legs hugging her sides, he let her pitch, and as soon as she found that he was there to stay she ceased bucking.

Sam headed her for Trabajo, hungry and sore and in a savagely vile mood. It was a mood, however, that the mare did not suspect, for not once had he cursed her or frightened her.

It was nine o'clock when he rode into town. Ahead of him, where the street opened up onto the plaza, he noticed that all the stores were lighted, and that there were many people on the street. Puzzled, he rode on, turning into the plaza and heading for the livery stable.

He was just past the corner when a man yelled, "There he is!"

Sam looked at the man and saw him whip out a six-gun and shoot. The mare grunted and went down, and Sam leaped clear. He had his mouth open to yell at the fool with the gun when another shot hammered out from the plaza. Something brushed against his Stetson.

For one second he looked around him; then, crouching low, he made a dash for the row of stores on the east side of the plaza. Men were running toward him from all directions.

He made the store front, yanked open the door, and ran in. He ran as far as the gun counter, leaped over it, grabbed a rifle and some shells, and ducked down behind the counter. The proprietor and clerks, all on the other side of the store, started taking pot shots at him just as the first man broke through the door. From an angle of the counter Sam emptied a whole chamber of shells at the floor in front of the door. Two men turned and ran out, but he could see them milling with the others on the sidewalk. The proprietor and clerks crawled toward the rear, and in another moment there was a pounding on the back door. It opened to let a dozen men in. They started to fire at the counter behind which he was hiding.

Sam lay there, listening to the boom of the slugs as they rapped against the wooden counter. What the hell, had the whole town gone crazy?

There came a lull in the firing and someone called out, "Surrender, Teacher, or we'll cut you to doll rags!"

"All right," Sam called.

"Throw that rifle out here and stand up. Come up hands first."

Sam did. Cautiously the groups from both the front and rear of the store approached him.

It was Sheriff Lovejoy, a shotgun in his hand, who searched him and then said, "All right, boys. Take him to the jail—and shoot the man who tries to stop you."

"Wait a minute," Sam said. "What am I—"

He got no further. Someone shoved him inside a circle of armed men who hustled him out into the street, cut across the plaza, and entered the sheriff's office with him. The Ortega county jail, which opened off the sheriff's office, was a six-cell building of rock construction. Sam was thrown into the first cell and the door clanged shut after him.

"Go out front," Sheriff Lovejoy told the others. "If a mob forms, break it up. Nothing is going to happen to this man except justice!"

The others went out and Sheriff Lovejoy turned to face Sam. He was an old man, leather-skinned and slow-moving and spare of frame, but there was an anger in his gray eyes that fairly blazed.

His voice, however, was surprisingly mild as he said, "You ain't got the brains they brag up for you, Teacher."

Sam grasped the bars in both his small hands. "Listen," he snarled. "Either the whole town's drunk or I'm crazy. Which is it? What am I here for?"

"You are Teacher, ain't you?"

"I never said I wasn't. Ask Pearly Gates. Now, what am

I here for?"

"They found him."

"Who? Gates?"

Lovejoy didn't answer immediately. Then he sighed and said, "All right, mister, if you want to play it that way, let's do it. But why don't you confess? Make it easier for both of us."

"Confess to what?"

Lovejoy said, "All right. You're charged with the murder of Steve Drury."

For a moment they watched each other. Sudden understanding came to Sam, and it fell with the weight of lead. His hands dropped from the bars.

"The murder of Steve Drury?" he asked slowly, eyeing the sheriff. "And how did I do it?"

"Gun. Yours. It's got your initials on it. We found it on the place where you scrapped. His rope was there, covered with blood. You'd fought and he'd licked you and tied you up, but you broke loose, got the gun, and shot him." Sheriff Lovejoy paused long enough to look at the great welt on Sam's face, the mark where Tex had hit him. Then his glance traveled to Sam's bloody wrists.

"I didn't do it," Sam said.

Lovejoy shrugged. "This fella told the house girl his name was Sam Teacher. He was small, about your size. Figure it out. I already have."

CHAPTER EIGHT

Sam turned his back on Lovejoy and went over to his cot and sat down, and the sheriff left. Sam sat with his head in his hands, staring at the floor. Santee Bales had sewed it up tight this time. With Sam's record known by everyone, with his mission known to the Governor, he had every card stacked against him. But that didn't bother him so much; it was what he was going to tell Matt Drury. Young Steve was no good and probably would have wound up in serious trouble, but no man deserved to die the way he had died.

He was roused from his meditation by the sound of the corridor door opening. Matt Drury and Pearly Gates stepped into the cell block and Pearly shut the door after them.

Sam looked over at Drury, studying his face, and at first found only angry misery reflected in it. But when Drury came closer to the bars and put both hands on them, Sam saw there was a rage inside the man that was almost choking him.

Pearly, seeing it too, said, "Easy, Matt."

"I'm all right," Drury said in a thick, tired voice. "I'm just wonderin' why I don't shoot you now, Teacher."

"You really think I killed Steve?"

"Why did you?" Drury said harshly. "Why did you have to? What did you want that you couldn't have got from me for the asking? Why did you have to do it?" His hands were grasping the bars until his knuckles showed white.

"Easy, Matt," Pearly said.

"I gave you a job when you asked for it. I gave you your

self-respect back. I even listened to you tell me what to do with my son and daughter. Now, my son's dead and my daughter has left me. Why did you do it?"

"Listen," Sam said, walking up to Drury, his glance level and angry. "If you want the whole story, Drury, here it is. Your son throwed in with Santee Bales—the biggest crook in the Territory. Do you know why Bales went in partnership with Steve? So he could get you to give Steve some land. And do you know what land you gave him? The canyon of Rio Medio—the canyon that the Southwestern and Rio Grande railroad has got to have for a way off the Ute Rim. Steve signed a partnership agreement with Bales. Bales killed him and by the agreement he gets the land. He'll sell it to the railroad in a week."

Drury didn't say anything for a moment. He looked at Sam, his gaze searching, skeptical. Presently, he said, "How do you know?"

Sam told him how, told him of his capture, of being held prisoner by Santee. As he talked he saw the iron disbelief mount in Drury's face.

When he finished, Drury said quietly, "You lie! The story out there is plain as day. You called him out of bed this morning. You took him out and tried to persuade him to break his partnership with Bales, probably to join you in robbing me of the canyon. He refused. You fought and he beat you and tied you up, intending to go after Bales. He even built a fire to make coffee—the can was still there by the fire. You broke loose and shot him and scared both the horses off when you shot. That's the true story, plain to a blind man." He pointed to Sam's wrists, then to his face. "Those marks say you killed my boy."

"You're a liar," Sam said.

"I think you're wrong, Matt," Pearly said.

"Right or wrong," Drury said in a strangely quiet voice, "I'm going to see you swing, Teacher, if it takes every cent I've got to buy a jury that will convict you!"

He turned and said, "Come on, Pearly," and they both went out, but not before Pearly had raised a hand to wave a good-by to Sam. Out in the office, Sheriff Lovejoy and four other men were waiting. They were respectfully grim.

"What do you want me to do with him, Matt?" Lovejoy asked.

"Guard him."

Lovejoy cleared his throat and drew uneasy circles on his desk top with a blunt finger, looking all the while at Drury. Finally he said, "Matt, I'm goin' to make you a proposition that I ought to be ashamed of, but I ain't." He stopped drawing the circles. "If you want, some of my men could stir up a mob that would lynch that little killer. All you got to do is give the word."

Pearly Gates said quickly, "That's a hell of a proposition to come from the mouth of a lawman!"

"So it is," Lovejoy said stubbornly. "But I mean it. There's no doubt in anybody's mind but what he's guilty. It'll be a month before he's tried. In that time, if he don't escape by himself, a gang of them outlaws may break him out of jail. And if he ever does come to trial, Matt, it's goin' to be the poor man agin' the rich man. You know that. He may go free."

"Justice don't count, I suppose," Pearly said dryly.

"It's justice he's goin' to git," Lovejoy said grimly. "At the end of a rope. He should of swung years ago. But he's always got out of it. I don't like to see him get out of this." He paused. "You just give the word, Matt."

"I'll see him tried, Anse," Drury said.

"*Maybe* you will," Lovejoy answered.

"Nevertheless, he'll get a trial, whether he deserves it or not."

Lovejoy nodded. "It's your boy he killed, Matt. You're the judge."

Drury said, "Thanks, anyway, Anse," and went out, Pearly following him. A crowd of the curious gathered around the sheriff's office watched Matt and Pearly climb into a buckboard. They called encouraging things—their sympathy, their anger, their good wishes—to Matt Drury, which he did not seem to hear. Pearly wheeled the buckboard around the plaza.

"Did you see Celia?" Drury asked in a dead voice.

"Yes. She—uh—she ain't feelin' well."

"You mean she doesn't want to see me, don't you?"

Pearly sighed. "That's it, I reckon."

"All right. Drive on out to the ranch."

Pearly didn't talk for a moment, and then he said gently, "Hell, Matt. You're doin' the right thing with her. Don't give up when you've gone this far."

"Right?" Drury murmured. "Don't forget it was suggested to me by that damned killer."

"You don't know he killed Steve," Pearly said.

"I do know it, by God!" Matt Drury said harshly.

"You got a gun, which was stole from him, and a rope that could have been bloodied, as the evidence. On the other hand, you got his story, which he can back up. If Bales sells that Rio Medio strip to the railroad, you got proof of his story right there."

"Only proof that Bales was after the right-of-way."

"Sam Teacher ain't a killer, Matt."

"His record proves you a liar, Pearly."

"Nevertheless," Pearly said stubbornly, "he ain't a killer."

Drury didn't answer. A little farther on, Pearly asked, "What are you goin' to do with him, Matt?"

"Teacher? Hang him."

"You can do it," Pearly admitted.

"Of course I can. I've never been so glad I had power as I am now. If influence won't do it, I'll buy his way to the gallows."

Pearly was quiet a long moment. "What about Celia, then?"

"I'm going down on my knees to her and ask her forgiveness," Drury said in a low voice. "I think she'll come back."

There was no more talk until they pulled into the plaza by the blacksmith shop at the Star 22.

Drury dismounted, and Pearly said, "Wait a minute, Matt." He was quiet a moment, framing what he was about to say, and Drury, standing by the front wheel, waited impatiently.

"This is hard, Matt," Pearly said. "I'm—I'm leavin'."

"Leaving the Star Twenty-Two?" Drury asked, after a moment's pause.

"That's right."

"Why?"

Pearly said quietly, "You and me ain't always seen eye to eye, but we have on the big things. This Sam Teacher business is a big thing, Matt—big to me. I don't like to see any man framed."

"I see," Drury said.

"Another thing is Celia. Whether Teacher killed Steve or didn't, he had the right idea on him and Celia. Right now, Celia is on the line, Matt. She can step one way or the other. If you leave her alone, stick to your word, chances are in a year she'll be the kind of girl we all want her to be. But if you ask her back, Matt, then you've hurt her so bad she'll never get over it."

"Hurt her?"

"Yes. Ain't it hurtin' a woman to give her more than the man she marries can ever hope to give her? Ain't it hurtin' her to make her so selfish that a man wouldn't even marry her? Ain't it hurtin' her to make her so used to winnin' every fight that she can't take a lickin' when one comes along? Ain't it?"

"If you're tryin' to make me desert her, Pearly, it won't work. I won't do it."

"I didn't expect you would." Pearly shook his head. "That's why you don't need me no more, Matt."

"But I do!"

"No, you're set on doin' two things that I can't go along with. You can walk that road alone, Matt. I'm quittin', while we still like each other. I can't help you no more."

Drury looked down at his feet, then, slowly, he looked up at his foreman.

"You've been a damn loyal friend, Pearly," he said.

"Sure I have. Hell, I still am. Only I'm provin' it my way, not yours."

"The job's here whenever you want it back."

"Thanks," Pearly said. "Nick Armbruster can run this outfit as well as me, Matt. Make him ramrod. I'll be moved out in a couple of days." He picked up the reins. "Good night."

"Good night."

Before sunup next morning, Pearly was on the road to Trabajo. Just at daylight he knocked on the door of the sheriff's office and was admitted by a sleepy but cautious guard. Pearly checked his gun, submitted to a search, and was then allowed to see Sam, who had been wakened by the talk. Pearly listened to Sam's story, down to the smallest detail, then left and rode out toward the Rio Medio. He rode hard. Once at the boulder field at the shoulder of the canyon, he picked up Sam's tracks. At the *rincon* he squatted on his haunches and studied it before entering. He saw many things there, and all fitted in with Sam's story, even to the coffee grounds powdering the dust at the base of the tree. Finished, he tracked Sam to the stream, then to the ford, and studied the place where Sam had roped the mare.

Satisfied, he rode back to town, arriving in late afternoon. He changed clothes then, barely in time to take his place in Steve Drury's funeral procession. He headed the Star 22 crew, which was there to a man. Celia Drury came with her father and left with him, but it signified nothing to Pearly, for she did not speak a word to her father. Afterward, back in town, Drury told Pearly he was riding out to the ranch with the rest of the crew. Pearly said he'd hang around town for a while.

Then he went back to the jail, submitted to the same examination, and joined Sam Teacher. This time he was admitted to the cell.

"Well?" Sam said.

"It's just like you said."

"How many men were there?"

"Two at the rocks, three at the *rincon.* They took your horse, too."

Sam nodded. Pearly was looking at him in a way that made him uneasy. "What's the matter?"

"There's only one thing about this I don't understand," Pearly said. "You ain't told it all, have you?"

"You could see the tracks for yourself."

"I don't mean that. I mean about why you come here in the first place." He paused. "Why did you?"

"I had a job."

"Sure. But why'd you get it? You and Bales knew each other before, or he wouldn't have bothered to show you that deed and the agreement. You'd talked about this right-of-way for the railroad before, hadn't you?"

Sam looked down at his hands. There was no longer any reason for secrecy, since the right-of-way was lost. Still, the fact that the Governor had backed him must be kept secret from Drury, and Pearly Gates was Drury's foreman.

He grinned at Pearly. "If you wasn't Drury's ramrod, Pearly, I might tell you. But you'd feel duty-bound to tell him, and I don't want that."

"I quit bein' Drury's foreman last night."

Sam hesitated. "What for?"

"I don't like to see an innocent man framed."

Sam said quietly, "Thanks."

"You want to tell me?"

Sam told him about the Governor's desire for both the railroad and Drury's friendship, and of the bargain he made with the Commissioner, of the amnesty and the price, and of Santee Bales's proposition that they go in partnership to double-cross the Governor.

When he was finished, Pearly rolled a smoke. "And all you get out of it now is hung, eh?"

"Looks that way."

"If you got out, what would you do?"

"If I still could," Sam said quietly, "I'd keep my word to

the Governor. But even if I couldn't, I'd kill Santee Bales."

"Which would you do first?"

"Keep my word to the Governor."

Pearly's mustache rose a little from the smile behind it. "I'm glad you said that." Then he rose, slapped Sam on the back, and left.

CHAPTER NINE

THE MORNING AFTER THE FUNERAL, Helen Barker was called to the door by a knock. Celia heard voices and afterward footsteps on the stairs and in the corridor that led to her room.

Helen appeared in the doorway and said, "Your father wants to see you. He's out on the porch."

"I don't want to see him," Celia answered.

Helen came into the room. She was a friendly girl with taffy-colored hair, a placid face, and an attractive smile. Celia was looking out the window, her back to the room, when she felt Helen's arm about her waist.

"It won't hurt to talk to him. Maybe he'll feel better. After all, he must be lonely."

"He should have thought of that before he drove us both out," Celia said bitterly.

"He's almost an old man," Helen said. "You don't have to agree with what he says. Just listen."

"We'll fight."

"I don't think so. He doesn't seem to be in a fighting mood."

Celia hesitated only a second and then said, "All right." She went downstairs and out onto the porch. Drury was sitting in the swing, and he came to his feet when he saw her. "Sit down, honey," he said.

Celia did—as far from him as she could get. Drury looked out at the street, chewing his lower lip, his hands smoothing his trousers.

"Pearly quit me today," he announced.

The news startled Celia into saying, "Pearly? Why? Did

you quarrel?"

"No, it was a friendly parting. He doesn't believe we're holding Steve's killer."

"He thinks somebody else did it, you mean?"

"Yes."

"And you fired him?"

"No. He just wanted to go." Suddenly Drury put his hand out and took Celia's. "Come back home, honey."

"No." Celia took her hand away.

"I'm sorry I was so bullheaded. I—I lost a son through it. I don't want to lose you."

"No."

"But everything will be the same. Your old room, your dresses, your maid. They're all trivial, honey. I'll double them. I'll give you anything you want."

"You can never take back what you said that day."

"I was angry."

"But you spoke your feelings, angry or not."

Drury lapsed into silence. He looked like a defeated and wornout old man, and for a moment Celia felt a pity for him. But then she thought of Steve, dead now—because of what her father had done.

Drury said, "Can't you forget that one day in your life, Celia? Just pretend it didn't happen?"

"Dad, of course I can forget that day. If you leave out what was said it was just another quarrel. But I can't come home knowing that you have more contempt than love for me."

"That's not so."

"It is so."

"Then you won't come?"

"No."

"How will you live?"

"I'll work."

Drury turned his head swiftly to look at her. "Where?"

"I don't know." Celia stood up, wanting to end this. "It's no use, Dad. When I left home I said I'd never come back. I never will."

Drury stood up and nodded. He looked long at her, said, "Good-by, dear," and stepped off the porch. Celia had a feeling of panic as she watched him mount and ride off, but it was only momentary. Slowly she went up to her room, confused and miserable. She felt she had to prove to her father that she wasn't what he believed her to be, and what Sam Teacher said she was. She wanted him to apologize, but the kind of an apology she had just received wasn't what she wanted. That only proved that her father loved her even if she wasn't worth it. And in these last three days she had come to believe that she wasn't worth it, and that what Sam Teacher had called her wasn't far from the truth. He had been right about Steve, she remembered. Now that Steve was gone she missed him, but she knew she had never had any real love or liking for him. Coldly and clearly she saw that Sam Teacher was right: Steve had been worthless, with nothing about him that was lovable. And if Teacher was right about Steve, why wasn't he right about her?

Helen was still there when Celia entered her room. "I'm leaving, Helen," Celia said.

"Going back? Good. I knew you'd patch it up."

"We haven't patched it up and I'm not going back," Celia said. "I'm going to work."

"But where?"

"I don't know. I'm going to get a job and then get a room and live by myself."

Helen came to her feet, amazement on her face. "But Celia, you can't! Think of your father!"

"I am."

"But what sort of work would you get? A servant's job? That's all women can do—that, and make hats or dresses."

"Oh, I don't *know,*" Celia said in a low voice. "But if I have to be a hired girl on somebody's ranch, I can do that. Let's don't talk about it."

"You're welcome to stay here as long as you want."

"Thanks. But I won't do it," Celia said, remembering with a kind of wry distaste what her father had said about wearing out her welcome. "I'm going job-hunting."

Walking down to the plaza under the shade of the big oaks that lined the street, she took stock of her resources. She had none—except a theoretical willingness to work. With a thoroughly feminine sense of reality, she knew that her looks, which never failed to attract men, and her size, which never failed to give them a desire to protect her, would be of no avail now.

And she was right. She told Harvey Miles, who owned the Emporium, that there were a hundred women who bought at his store. Then why shouldn't he hire a woman clerk, who could understand their wants and please them? Miles was an opinionated man; it showed in his close-set eyes which shuttled between easy tolerance and suspicion. He told her that she was right, but that for every yard of dress goods he sold to women, men bought fifty pairs of Levi's; for every sack of flour bought by a woman, the ranches bought two barrels. No, this was a man's store, where men loafed, swore, swapped yarns, and bought supplies. A woman would drive them off. If it was money she wanted, he'd loan her any amount she wanted.

She tried the Elite with the same lack of success. She turned to the hotel, and was refused because all the work there was too menial. It did her no good to argue that menial work was what she wanted; Ben Luckman only laughed and refused.

On the street again, she felt frightened and desperate. For the first time in her life she realized that she had nothing to market, that she was a woman and therefore at a disadvantage when it came to earning a living, and that unless she wanted to swallow her words and go back to her father, she would have to break down this barrier.

It was then that she saw the sign on Double-Jack Jackson's Gem Café. Double-Jack had driven a Star 22 roundup wagon for fifteen years before he had saved the money to buy this restaurant. She had ridden many a day on the seat of the chuck wagon beside him.

Double-Jack's Gem Café was a narrow room with a line

of stools and a counter on one side, and two tables on the other, the last to bear out the sign on his window: *Tables for Ladies.*

He was a grouchy-looking man to a stranger, with his bald head and its thin saddle of dry gray hair, his yellow, impatient face, and his truculent eyes. Celia, however, was not awed; she knew that all ranch cooks were savage-looking, enormous drinkers, and really gentle men.

Double-Jack came out of the kitchen at her entrance, rubbing his hands on his apron. He wouldn't speak of Steve, she knew, because he had been to the funeral and would consider it an ample concession to the decencies.

She took a stool, and he said, "No jelly-cake, sis. But I got the sinkers you like."

"Hello, Double-Jack. It's not food today."

"Not hungry?"

"All right. Doughnuts and coffee."

Double-Jack got two cups of coffee and a plate of doughnuts and they both ate, he from his side of the counter, Celia from her stool. When she had praised his cooking, which was really good, and he had admitted it, she said, "I want a job, Double-Jack."

He glared at her with mock ferociousness. "Punchin' cattle, maybe."

"No, I mean it."

"Row with Matt?"

Celia nodded. "This time for good. I'm out on my own, and I have to support myself."

"Make hats," Double-Jack said. "I can give you the fried eggs to paste on 'em."

"Be serious. I want to work here."

Double-Jack had a cup of coffee halfway to his mouth. He set it down slowly and said, "What?"

"I can wait table. I can make change. I can learn enough about cooking to make the coffee and the pastry. Besides that, you need someone."

"Supposin' I do. I don't need you."

"What's the matter with me?"

"Nothing, only—why, hell, you're Matt Drury's daughter."

Celia put both elbows on the counter. "If a strong, healthy girl, willing to work, a girl you knew you could get on with and who liked you, stepped up to your counter today and asked you for a job, would you give it to her?"

"I reckon," Double-Jack said cautiously.

"Then forget about Dad. I'm dead serious about needing money and work and a place to live. And I'll *work*, too."

"I'll pay twenty a month and food. Where'll you live if you get the job?"

"I don't know. But I'll find a place."

"There's a storeroom up above the café here, and it's only got one entrance, through the kitchen. Reckon you could clean it up and use it?"

"You mean you'll give me work?"

"That's what I'm sayin', ain't it?" Double-Jack shook his head. "Hell, I've had a Drury around me half my life. I might's well keep one around for the rest of it."

Celia leaned over and kissed his bald head, and Double-Jack grinned. But as she went out, his face settled into gravity again. It looked to him like he'd made a bad deal. She was a little hellion from the word go, never done a lick of work in her life. If she decided she liked the sound of plates breaking, she'd drop a hundred of them on the floor just for fun. He shrugged and turned back into the kitchen. After all, Matt Drury had been his bread and butter for fifteen years, and damn good bread and butter, too. He guessed he could do that much for him—and besides, hellion or no hellion, he liked Celia.

Celia was happy as she walked down the street. Pearly Gates was standing on the step of the small saddle shop that adjoined the sheriff's office and the jail.

She came up to him, and he took off his hat, grinning.

"Dad said you quit, Pearly."

"Unh-hunh. I'm wore out. Takin' a rest."

"Because you think Sam Teacher didn't kill Steve?"

"That'll do for an excuse, sure."

Celia studied his face, and he avoided her eyes. "That's the first wrong guess you ever made, Pearly."

"It ain't even a guess," Pearly said quietly.

"I hope they hang him," she said quietly.

Pearly shifted his feet and didn't say anything. Celia told him about her job, and Pearly grunted approval.

"Come and help me move, Pearly," she invited him.

"This afternoon," Pearly said. "Frank's goin' to dinner in a minute."

"Frank who?"

Pearly jerked a thumb over his shoulder toward the door of the saddle shop. "Frank Baker."

"What if he is? Are you watching the shop?"

"That's right." Pearly's ragged mustache moved a little in a grin. "I own the place now."

"The saddle shop?"

Pearly nodded. "Bought it this mornin'. I got to do something, and I know more about saddles than anything else, includin' cows and murders."

They talked a minute until Frank Baker, the harness maker, stepped out. Celia went on upstreet, and Pearly walked back into the shop. He shut the door and locked it and pulled the blind. Then he went back through the shop, past the harness hanging on long wooden pegs, past the saddles thrown over sawhorses, past the benches littered with tools at the rear. The shop was cool, smelling of leather and grease and dust and horses.

Against the rear wall there was a trap door in the floor. Pearly opened it and went down the stairs. He found a lantern sitting on the third step from the bottom, and he lighted it before going on into the cellar. Carefully, then, amid the clutter of barrels, boxes, bottles, old stoves, old magazines, old lumber that littered the cellar, he started his business. His back against the front wall, he counted off sixteen paces toward the stairs. Then he did it again, to make sure. After that, he marked the place on the wall next to the jail. Satisfied, he took off his vest, put his watch and the lantern on a barrelhead, then picked up a pickax, a sledge, a cold chisel, and a shovel which were at the foot of the stairs.

He went to work then, prizing out a hole in the stone foundation of the shop. He was working on the wall which was next to the jail.

Pearly had learned one thing in his visit to Sam Teacher. The cell Sam was in was sixteen paces from the boardwalk on the street. And it had an earthen floor.

CHAPTER TEN

SAM TEACHER had been in jail for a week. His preliminary hearing had been short and to the point. He was charged with first-degree murder, and his plea was "not guilty." It was put before the preliminary hearing by a long-haired drunken lawyer who had been given the case and who could not stay awake long enough to get his whole story.

The outlook was hopeless, he could see. He already had been tried, condemned to death, and hanged in the minds of these people. His single friend, Pearly Gates, had not been in for five days, and Sam remembered bitterly his telling Pearly about the Governor's business. Either Pearly had gone back to the Star 22, or he had lied to Sam about quitting, or he had let the sentiment of the town scare him away. Of all the things that had happened to him since he had come to this country, Pearly's desertion was the most bitter. But why had he done it? Was he convinced, in spite of what he had seen, that Sam had murdered young Drury?

His temper wore thin during that week, and he could not eat. Once he threw his food in the face of the jailer, and two deputies had come back and beaten him up. Even that had been a relief. The other inmate of the jail, a loudmouthed, bragging puncher accused of rustling cattle, spent all his waking moments riding Sam, tell him he was sure to be convicted, taunting him for being a yellow-bellied bushwhacker.

He smoked cigarette after cigarette, trying to shut his ears to the yapping of the puncher. Finally, when he could stand it no longer, he would get up and grab hold of the bars and call the puncher every name he could think of, his voice shaking with rage. The puncher would laugh at him and begin all over again.

He was lying on his cot just after supper this evening, watching the night steal in through his window, blotting out the square of dusk. He was waiting for resignation to come, but it would not. He kept studying the mortar of the stone walls, the bars, the ceiling, thinking of escape. But any escape now was impossible under the eyes of the puncher. His every move was watched, commented on.

It was quiet here now, but his mind was racing. Suddenly he heard a muffled tapping. He propped himself up on his elbow, listening.

The puncher, two cells away, was watching him in the dusk.

"Lie down, mister," the puncher jeered. "Better start gettin' used to a space six by three. You'll lie in one until eternity."

Sam said, "Die in the night, will you?" and lay down again. But there was still the tapping, and now it was getting more and more distinct. He got off the cot and walked to the window to listen. It was so muffled that he knew the puncher could not hear it. He was standing there, his head turned to listen, when he heard the sudden rustle of dirt slipping. Swiftly he looked around him, and saw the dirt of the floor, about three feet square, sag some more and then slip and drop.

A hole appeared in the floor.

"Sam," he heard a voice say. The puncher heard it, too. He lunged off his cot to listen.

Sam dropped to his knees and peered down into the hole. There was a lantern down there, and Pearly Gates was holding it, looking up at him. He was six feet below, Sam judged.

"Come on!" Pearly said. "Hurry it up!"

Suddenly the puncher began to bawl at the top of his lungs, "Help! Help! Escape!"

Sam laughed at him. A pencil of light from the corridor door appeared on the floor as Sam slipped down into the hole and dropped. He found himself in the tunnel, and Pearly, swearing, was ahead of him.

"Hurry," Pearly said, crawling on his hands and knees.

The cellar, Sam saw in his brief glance around, was almost full of the loose dirt that Pearly had brought out of the tunnel.

"Horses out in the alley!" Pearly said. "Drag it, son. We ain't got much time!"

"We got enough for me to do a little errand," Sam said grimly. "Give me your gun."

"But—"

"Gimme it!"

Pearly, as he ran across to the stairs, unbuckled his shell belt and gun and gave them to Sam. They mounted the stairs and at the head of them Sam said, "I'll meet you in the alley."

"Don't be a damn fool!" Pearly said. "Come—" But Sam was gone.

Once in the street, he raced the ten steps to the sheriff's office, lunged through the cell-block door, and hauled up, his gun leveled. Inside, Sheriff Lovejoy and the two deputies were trying with nervous hands to fit the key to his cell in the lock.

"Stay right put," Sam said quietly.

"There he is now!" the puncher bawled.

The sheriff and his two deputies raised their hands. Lovejoy said bitterly, "Damn you, Teacher, did you come back to kill us, too?"

"You, sheriff, unlock the door to Loudmouth's cell." The sheriff obeyed with alacrity. "Now get in, all of you."

"You can't do that!" Lovejoy said.

"Will you get in there, you three, or do I have to slug you and throw you in?"

The two deputies followed Lovejoy into the cell. Sam locked the door and took the keys.

"Take a good look at it," Sam said. "I roosted in one of

the damn things for a week."

"I'll be out of here in a day!" Lovejoy raged.

"If you are, I'll come back and throw you in again."

"You come back here again and we'll hang you, Teacher."

"I'll be back," Sam drawled. "You're goin' to serve your time in there like I did. One whole week. Seven days. Remember that, you bunch of tinhorn wrong-guessers, the next time you throw an innocent man in there. Because I'm goin' to show you what a week in jail means."

Lovejoy started to yell. Sam heard the pounding of feet on the boardwalk outside, and unlocked the door to his own cell. Waving in mock salute to the three men in the cell, he then lowered himself into the hole again, crawled through to the cellar, mounted the stairs, went out the back door, and found Pearly in the alley, holding both horses.

"What in—"

"Ride," Sam said. "I'll tell you later."

He and Pearly rode north out of town, taking to the creek at a slow pace so as to make little noise. Upstream, they paused and heard the town below them come awake. Men were yelling out in the plaza. A couple of signal shots were let loose in the air. Sam grinned into the night, spurred his horse, and then took a dozen deep breaths of free air. They clung to the Rio Arriba for a mile.

Then Sam said, "Nobody's seen you, Pearly. You better let me go on alone."

"No."

"You'll be outlawed," Sam said.

"I will be anyway," Pearly said. He told Sam of his purchase of the saddle shop. When the tunnel was discovered it would be apparent to Sheriff Lovejoy who had dug it.

When he was finished Sam said, "You mean you put out three thousand dollars for that saddle shop, just so's you could break me out?"

"I still own it."

"You did that and you broke me out of jail and you're

an outlaw now. Why, Pearly?"

"I don't like to see an innocent man framed," Pearly said patiently.

"I'm used to this, Pearly. You ain't. From now on, besides havin' a price on my head, I'm goin' to ride high, wide, and handsome. I'm goin' to take chances only a fool would take. I'll likely have the army on my trail in another month. I won't eat regular and I won't sleep regular and I'll wear out a couple of saddles. I'm goin' to tear this Territory wide open. You still want to stick with me?"

"That's why I broke you out."

"Then let's ride," Sam said. "You find us a hidin' place. I'll take care of the rest of it."

CHAPTER ELEVEN

PURSUIT, of course, was inevitable, and Pearly set out to shake the posse which would be on their trail by morning. It was a task he could concentrate on with relish, for he knew every foot of this vast range. Every stream, every patch of malpais, every stray band of horses helped to cover their tracks. Doubling back and circling, and cutting their own trail innumerable times, he steadily worked north toward the rim. At noon, they climbed to the rim by a narrow cattle trail, and by midafternoon were in a lonely canyon of the Ute foothills. Pearly chose the hiding place with foresight. At first sight it appeared to be a dry and inaccessible place, twisting tortuously into the foothills. But deep in it there was a small cave, and less than a quarter-mile from the cave there was a spring which welled out of a limestone outcropping, flowed a hundred feet to make a minute patch of the canyon floor green with grass, and then disappeared again into the ground.

Food, blankets, and ammunition were all wrapped in the slickers behind their saddles, and just at nightfall they dismounted, made their camp, staked out their horses up the canyon close to the spring, and ate.

Once the job of guiding them to a safe hiding place was over, Pearly seemed to be at a loss. Their supper of pan bread, jerky, and coffee finished, they rolled smokes and lay back on their blankets before the cave. Sam was quiet, his face creased by a scowl. Pearly wanted to talk, but something on Sam's face told him that it wouldn't be welcome.

Suddenly Sam said, "Santee will be up here from Santa

Luz in a couple of days, Pearly. We got to work fast."

"Work fast at what?"

"Gettin' that right-of-way from him."

"It's got," Pearly said. "That's the only thing we can't change, Sam."

"We got to."

"But he's likely struck a bargain with the Governor or the railroad already. It's out of his hands."

Sam smoked thoughtfully for a moment and then said, "Somethin' keeps stickin' in my mind, Pearly. I can't get it out."

"What?"

"When Santee showed me the deed to the Rio Medio canyon, he asked me if I knew where the east boundary of the Ortega grant was. Where is it?"

"The Rio Medio canyon."

"But the words. What are the words of the old charter?"

Pearly thought a minute, and then said, "I can't say 'em exact. But it's something like, 'The east boundary of said grant shall be three hundred varas at all points east of the river known as the Rio Medio.' "

"You sure it says the *river?*"

"Sure. What else could the Rio Medio be? *Rio* is Spanish for river."

Sam asked about the other boundaries then, but he wasn't paying attention to what Pearly said.

Then Sam asked a question that seemed completely irrelevant. "Drury ever had his land surveyed?"

"No."

Sam sat up, dropping his cigarette. "You mean it's on the records just the way you told me?"

"Why not? The Ortega grant was here long before this was United States Territory. It was here long before it was the Republic of Mexico's Territory. It's been here since this was New Spain. Same boundaries, no bigger or no smaller. I don't reckon there's much sense in havin' it surveyed. The old Ortega charter is on file for anyone that wants to see it." He looked over at Sam, sensing the excitement in Sam's voice. "Why?"

"I'll tell you tomorrow. In the mornin' we're goin' to ride out and take a look at this country."

That was all Pearly was able to get out of him that evening. Next morning Sam was up and the fire was built before daylight. He went about the chores of camp whistling and humming, and Pearly, wondering at it, said nothing.

Breakfast finished, Sam said, "I'd like a look at the Rio Medio canyon, Pearly—the upper canyon."

"There's a posse out for us, son. We better hole up for a stretch."

"This can't wait," Sam said. "You comin', or am I goin' to do it alone?"

"You ain't goin' to do it alone," Pearly said grimly.

They saddled up and Pearly, again in the lead, headed east for the Rio Medio. They clung to the lower slopes of the foothills, ready, in case they sighted riders to the south on the long slope to the rim, to dodge back into the foothills. But Pearly had worked better than he knew in covering their tracks. The posse was still tangled up and baffled by the story of the tracks below the rim.

The northeast corner of the Ortega grant lay right at the base of the long, twisted mesas that made up the Ute foothills. The Rio Medio, riding a fairly deep canyon, rushed out of the foothills at this corner, and Sam, taking the lead now, turned up the canyon. For four hours he rode without bothering to look at the canyon walls, but when, sometime in early afternoon, the canyon gave way to the base of the mountains, he began to look around. Pearly, watching him, could make no sense of what he was doing.

When at last they came to a great shoulder of rock that joined the base of the mountain, Sam pointed to the other side of the canyon and said. "Let's see what's over the hump."

What was over the hump, and directly over it, was another canyon. For some reason, this seemed to interest

Sam. "Let's ride down it," he suggested.

"But we just come up this one," Pearly objected.

"Sure. Only I'm curious."

Pearly sighed and pulled his horse in behind Sam's. The rest of the afternoon, Pearly almost drowsed in his saddle. Here between the high walls of this dry canyon, without a drop of water on its floor to cool the air, it was like a furnace. Sam, however, was alert and curious. He kept watching the sun and taking directions, and when, almost at dusk, they came out of the foothills again, he waited for Pearly to come up to him. "How far to the Rio Medio?" he asked.

"Along the base of these mesas?" When Sam nodded, Pearly said indifferently, "Ten, fifteen miles."

Sam threw a leg over his saddle horn and contemplated Pearly, who was swabbing the sweat from his forehead with the back of his sleeve.

"Pearly, we need tools."

"Tools?"

"A drill and a sledge. Two drills and two sledges."

"What for?"

A faint grin creased Sam's face as he looked off at the plains, now touched a golden yellow by the last rays of the sun. "Well, I'll tell you . . ."

It was two nights later that Sam and Pearly paused at the bridge of the Rio Arriba just above Trabajo. It was dark where they pulled up at the bridgehead, but across the stream and up the short winding road to the shelf on which the town lay, the lamps were lighted and there were the usual night sounds of a town that has not yet gone to bed.

"I don't like it," Pearly said.

Sam laughed quietly.

"You can laugh," Pearly murmured, "but think, son. There's two roads out of town. One is this one. The other pulls up from the town slope onto the plain. All they got to do is bottle up them roads and you're caught."

"We got out the night you broke me out of jail."

"Before they knowed what had happened. This time, they'll damn well know. You warned 'em you'd be in again."

Sam said, "Sure I did. Because I aim to come again and again."

"I don't like it," Pearly repeated.

Sam shifted in his saddle. "I ain't worried about how I'll come out. It's you."

"There'll be thirty buckboards in that damn town," Pearly said resentfully. "They ain't goin' to chase you in a buckboard. I can get one of 'em."

"All right. But what about the store?"

"Take my word for it. Harvey Miles never missed any hell-raisin' in his life. The minute you start curlin' your tail, he'll send his help home, lock up, and join the hunt."

"You know that?"

"Hell, didn't I see him do it the day they found young Steve's body? I'm tellin' you, he'd ride out with a posse if he was in a nightshirt."

Sam lifted his reins and said, "All right. This is Thursday. I'll likely see you Saturday."

"If your luck holds out," Pearly said gloomily. "Look, Sam, why—"

"I'm goin'," Sam said. He touched his pony into a walk, and Pearly sighed.

"All right, damn it. Only, I'm too old to do things like this, son. And you're too young."

"We're both just right."

At the top of the short hill, they could look down the street that opened onto the plaza. Sam, with a careless wave of his hand, turned into the alley that would lead him through other alleys, past the back end of the jail. Pearly shook his head and murmured, "Good luck, kid," and then rode on to a dark corner of the plaza.

He dismounted and pulled his horse over to a tie rail. A few people loafed on the sidewalks under the wooden awnings. He noted idly that there were a dozen buckboards with teams around the square. There were also about fifty saddle horses. That would make a sizable posse, Pearly thought, and he wiped his forehead with his handkerchief. Now he was looking at the saddle shop, his own saddle shop. That was where it would happen.

He stared at the dark doorway until his eyes hurt. And then he saw it. A slight, lazily arrogant figure stepped out of the doorway, turned upstreet, and paused at the doorway of the sheriff's office where the windows were lighted.

Sam hesitated only long enough to pull his gun, then he opened the door and stepped inside, closing it in the same fluid motion. When he came to a stop, his gun was hip-high, pointed at Sheriff Lovejoy. Talking with the sheriff, who was seated at his desk, was a deputy, one of Sam's former jailers.

"Howdy," Sam said.

For a moment Lovejoy only stared at him, then he made a move to rise. Sam didn't say anything; he simply cocked the gun in his hand. Its sound was enough to change Lovejoy's mind. He sat down again.

"I thought I took care of you the other night," Sam said to the deputy. "What's the matter? Did they have an extra set of keys?"

"I dunno what you're talkin' about," the deputy said.

Sam put out a hand. "Hand 'em over, mister."

The deputy rose to his feet, his face red. "Not me, you cocky little—"

Sam took one step forward and hit him in the face. The deputy staggered into Lovejoy, tripped on the sheriff's feet, and fell against the wall, then sat down.

"That's just part payment for that beatin' I got under the gun of your pardner last week, mister." He put out his hand again. "Now I'll take that extra set of keys."

Lovejoy said, "By God, you can drive a man too far."

Sam's cold gaze whipped up to Lovejoy's face. "That's right. Funny you never realized that with me, sheriff. I'm the man that's been drove too far." He smiled unpleasantly. "Now do I get them keys or do I have to make you both undress and walk buck naked outside so's I can search your clothes?"

"We have men with rifles planted in every store on the plaza," Sheriff Lovejoy said. "You can't get away with it, Teacher."

"The keys."

The jailer reached in his pocket and brought out a large key ring holding six keys. Sam took them, saying, "Now get inside."

He prodded them both back to the end cell where the rustler was and opened the door. "You're goin' to have company for a stretch, Big Wind," he told the surprised rustler. "I'm coming' back again, about the time they saw you out. Now don't forget it."

The deputy and Lovejoy cursed in level, measured violence, and Sam slammed the corridor door upon them. Once in the office again, he looked around him. A reward poster on the sheriff's desk attracted his attention and he walked over to read it. It was new, the ink scarcely dry, and it said: *$5000 reward, dead or alive,* on the top line. Below it was a picture of himself. It gave his name, description, and the latest crime of which he was guilty, the murder of Stephen Drury. Below it was printed: *This man is armed at all times, and is the most notorious pistol-shot in the Territory. Great caution should be exercised in his capture.*

But what made Sam smile until his lips were faint, thin lines over his teeth was the signature. It was that of a U.S. marshal. He picked up the dodger in a swift scooping motion and crumpled it. If any seal was needed to his death warrant, it was not lacking now.

Santee had got to the Governor, all right, with his right-of-way, and the Governor had believed Sam's guilt in Drury's murder too.

He holstered his six-gun then and pulled down a rifle and a box of shells from the gun rack. Then he blew the lamp, hoisted the shade and then the window, and knelt behind them, levering a shell into the gun. He'd give them a night they wouldn't forget for a long time!

He took a sight on the window of the first store on the north side of the plaza and fired. The light went out. Somebody yelled. He moved his gun muzzle on down the line of stores. Wherever there was a lamp in sight, he shot it out. From there he turned to the east side of the plaza and calmly, one by one, extinguished the lamps.

There was bedlam across the street now. From half a dozen different points the orange-purple wink of gun flames bloomed in the night. Men were yelling at each other, and he could see them running on the far sidewalk.

It was time to move, he knew, but not yet time to go. He slipped out the door, took the ten steps running to Pearly's saddle shop, then dodged in the door. On his way through the shop he picked up a lariat that lay coiled on the bench and a small crowbar beside it which he had placed there on his first visit.

Once in the saddle, he rode down the alley and turned right at the street heading onto the plaza. Already men were streaking across the plaza toward the sheriff's office, taking to the cover of trees and bushes as they moved ahead.

Touching spurs to his horse, he pointed him straight at the sidewalk. The horse took the two-foot jump to the level of the sidewalk at a dead run and then his feet began to thunder on the boardwalk under the awnings. Sam held the crowbar in his left hand, like a child running along a picket fence with a stick in his hand. Holding the crowbar out against the window fronts, he spurred his horse on. Window after window collapsed in a great bell-like jangle behind him as he rode the sidewalk clear down the north side of the plaza. At the northeast corner he kept going east and disappeared behind the buildings. The men in the plaza were now shooting at this corner.

Sam pulled his horse up sharply, slid out of the saddle, took his lariat out, joined it to the one he had brought, and then tied one to a hitching post at the corner. He trailed it across the street, pulled it waist high, and tied it to another hitching post, Just as he was finished, the first horseman thundered around the corner.

The pony hit the rope, stopped, and the rider sailed over his head. Sam mounted, rode on, turned left at the first alley, left again, then kept his course straight west behind the stores headed for the west road. As he climbed up the low hill that would bring him onto the plain above, he heard men talking ahead of him.

Rising in his saddle, he yelled, "Come on. He's gone out over the bridge!" Turning around in the dark, he galloped off down the hill for fifty yards, then pulled over off the road. In a moment, a half-dozen horsemen boiled down the hill past him. From his eminence now he could see the tangle of horsemen at the northeast corner of the plaza, and he smiled a little.

Then he pulled out his carbine and started laying shots over their heads. They milled for perhaps half a minute, then started out toward him, headed for the west road. Sam spurred his horse, achieved the top of the hill, and paused to listen. If he wanted them to keep on his trail, he would have to wait a moment. Just as they came pouring up onto the plain, he put two more shots over their heads, then swung his horse south in a long, easy lope.

When Pearly, who had watched all this from the southwest corner of the plaza, saw the posse head up the west road and heard the two shots from the top of the hill, he sat down to quiet his shaking knees. A dozen times this night he had thought that Sam was trapped. And when he rode the sidewalk down the whole north side of the plaza, crashing the window fronts as he progressed, Pearly had thought he had lost his mind.

Now that it was over, he remembered his job. He had not forgotten himself so far as to neglect watching the front of Harvey Miles's Emporium. And true to his hunch, Harvey had shut up store and taken the first horse he could find at the tie rail in front of his store. The Emporium was dark now, with not so much as a lamp burning. What few women were in town lined the sidewalks.

All the men, those who had horses and those who could get them at the livery stable, had left. Except for the women and old men, the town was deserted.

Pearly strolled unconcernedly over to a strange team hitched to a buckboard, untied them, mounted the seat, backed out, and headed out the northeast corner of the plaza. But once out of the square, he took to the alley that led him to the rear of the Emporium.

Half a dozen sheds faced the alley. With a bar of steel he pried the lock off the one that was used as a storeroom. Only when he had a dozen heavy cases packed and roped in the buckboard did he head north out of town, unrecognized.

CHAPTER TWELVE

SANTEE BALES, in company with a heavy-set, prosperous-looking stranger, arrived in town Saturday in a brand-new buggy. His first act was to register himself and his friend, who looked tired and worn, at the hotel; his second was to buy a half-dozen nine-inch cigars. With one of his new purchases jutting ahead of his clipped mustache, he set out for the sheriff's office. Prosperity had come to Santee Bales. His suit was of a quality which he could never have afforded before; in the holster on his hip his old gun was now furbished with ivory butt plates.

He found the sheriff's office deserted, but the door to the cell block was open and he heard sounds of activity in there. Entering, he saw something he did not immediately understand. Sitting on the floor before a cell, a hacksaw in his hand, a hundred blades spread out fanwise around him, was a blacksmith, and he was working on one of the bars. Inside the cell were Sheriff Lovejoy, in shirt sleeves, and two other men.

Santee walked up to the cell, removing his Stetson. "Sheriff Lovejoy?"

Lovejoy, looking weary and disgusted and faintly embarrassed, said, "Yes."

"I'm Santee Bales. Is it true that my partner, Stephen Drury, was murdered while I was gone?"

Lovejoy's interest picked up then. He rose and came over, and Santee put out his hand. They shook hands, Santee's face reserved and a little sorrowful.

"That's right," Lovejoy said.

"I also heard that you might want to see me for questioning. Was it in connection with the murder? And, by the way, who committed the murder?"

"Sam Teacher."

"Ah."

"You know him?"

"Who doesn't? A wolf, sir, a wolf."

Santee brought out one of his cigars and tendered it to the sheriff, who accepted it and a light for it.

"There was some talk of your connection with young Drury, Bales. But I got to admit most of it come from Teacher," Lovejoy said.

"That's all right," Santee said openly. "I had plenty of connection with young Drury. We were partners in a scheme to get a right-of-way for the railroad through Matthew Drury's land."

"That's what Teacher accused you of."

"Accused?" Santee's eyebrows rose. "That word has an unpleasant sound, as if you were speaking of a crime. If you call bringing a railroad into this Territory a crime, then I plead guilty to it. Gladly."

"But what about the horse ranch?" Lovejoy asked.

Santee smiled pityingly. "Sir, when you are putting through a hundred-thousand-dollar deal, you don't do it publicly. That talk was meant to cloud the issue."

"That's what young Steve told his dad, so he'd get the land."

"Of course he did," Santee agreed blandly. "Mr. Drury is not a believer in progress. He would strangle this Territory if he could. Young Steve knew it, and he sent for me. I have the Governor's ear. He had *his* governor's ear." Santee smiled at his little joke. "We were the ideal partners to swing a deal which would mean everlasting prosperity for this Territory. And it's swung, sheriff."

"You mean the railroad is comin' through?"

"I do. I have their representative with me at the hotel. Today he goes out to look at the right-of-way. If he approves of it, he pays me tonight. Next week the surveyors come." He nodded his head. "It means, sheriff, that at last this fair land has come into its own. There will be work for everybody; food will be cheaper; freight will be a tenth of what it is; all the small ranchers can ship now, whereas before they could not afford to drive. In short, it means gold and jobs and prosperity."

"I can see that," Lovejoy said, with the manner of a man asserting his belief in the eternal verities, "but what I'd like to have cleared up is Teacher's connection with all this. Why did he kill Drury? We know he did, but what was his motive?"

"Simple, sir. He wanted to be partners with young Drury. Steve wouldn't have anything to do with him. He probably called young Drury out for a last talk, was refused, lost his head, and killed him."

"Unh-hunh. That's what we figured."

"A sad story," Santee murmured. "Well, sheriff, when this deal is finished I'll deposit Steve Drury's share in the bank at Santa Luz. I suppose it will go to Matt Drury, who don't need it a tenth as much as young Steve did. But then, that's luck, eh?" He put out his hand. and the sheriff took it. "By the way, what are you doing in here?"

"Sam Teacher," Lovejoy said wryly, "busted in Thursday night and locked us in our own jail. He's got both sets of keys now, so we got to saw through this tool steel. We got a posse out after him."

"A wolf, that Teacher. Well, good day, sheriff. I'll be dropping in again."

Outside, Santee congratulated himself. On the theory that the best defense is a good offense, he had told Lovejoy just enough of the truth to win a staunch friend. Moreover, the sheriff had a respect for his brains, and that amounted to a lot more than a respect for his strength or his prowess with a gun. Walking over to the livery stable to rent horses, he felt well satisfied with himself. He had pulled a slick bit of business, had made the Governor knuckle under to him, had successfully outlawed Sam Teacher by saddling him with a murder, and now he stood to get a cold seventy-five thousand dollars, the top figure the railroad would pay.

He found the Southwestern and Rio Grande agent, Ross Colver, washed and waiting for him at the hotel. They mounted their two horses and started out for the Rio Medio, Santee expansive and in the best possible mood.

When they came to the mouth of the canyon in early afternoon, Santee pulled up on the rise and looked down at the canyon. "Well, sir," he said to Colver, "there's the promised land. And it's got a grade that your oldest engine could back up."

Colver laughed. "The only one in a couple of hundred miles, too."

Slanting down into the valley, Santee talked of many things. He was still talking when they came to the stream at the ford where they would cross to the other side.

Santee was talking price to Colver when he observed the expression in Colver's face. Then Colver pulled up and Santee pulled up and Colver said, "Look at that creek."

Santee swiveled his head to look. There was no water in it.

Where a rushing little river had been a week ago, there was now nothing but a dry stream bed. Only where the deepest pools had been was there any water, and there a bare bucket of it stood glassily reflecting the sky.

Santee stared at it with blank incomprehension. "Where the hell is the water?"

"That was a pretty wide creek, wasn't it?" Colver asked.

"But the water," Santee repeated. "Where is it?"

They both looked at it for a full minute, and then Colver turned his head to regard Santee. There was a look of shrewdness on his fat face as he observed, "This is supposed to be the Rio Media, is it?"

"Sure."

"All right. Where is it?"

"I don't know. That's the canyon, though. That's all you need to worry about."

"Oh, no, it isn't!" Colver said smoothly. "It isn't all you

need to worry about, either, Bales. That canyon doesn't concern me. The river does."

Santee's glance whipped up to Colver's face. "What do you mean?"

"I mean that the boundary of this grant—the piece you want to sell me that adjoins the boundary—is three hundred yards east of the Rio Medio—the Rio Medio *river,* that is, not the canyon. Where is the river?"

"But here's your right-of-way!"

"The only right-of-way you can sell me, my friend, starts three hundred yards east of the Rio Medio *river.* It runs west three miles. It runs north and south for twenty. I know that because I looked up the east boundary of the Ortega grant at the land office in Santa Luz. Now find me the Rio Medio—the river."

"But here it is!"

Colver shook his head. "This doesn't look like a river to me."

"It's a dry season," Santee said.

"It's a wet season, and you know it."

"Maybe the river has shifted its course. Let's look." Santee crossed the river bed and headed east. If the river had shifted its course only a mile or so east he was safe. If more, then he was out of luck—and he was also out of luck if it had shifted west. But a mile to the east there was no river. Santee pulled up his horse and looked at the country, his eyes dull with the knowledge that unless he could explain the unexplainable, unless he could find the Rio Medio, raise it, move it, bring it back to its old course, he was lost.

"You might look west of the canyon," Colver suggested.

"A hell of a lot of good that will do!" Santee said savagely. "That won't take in the canyon."

"That's true."

Santee turned to him. "Look here, Colver. Are you serious about this? Are you sure the charter said three hundred yards east of the Rio Medio *river,* not the Rio Medio canyon?"

"My dear sir," Colver said patiently. "I have bought rights-of-way for ten years. Do you think I don't look into the title and description of property before I put out seventy-five thousand dollars for it?"

"You've got to have the *river?*" Santee insisted.

"That's the legal boundary. Yes."

Santee said grimly, "You go back to town. I'm going to find that damn river. A river don't dry up overnight."

Colver shrugged. "All right. I'll wait a day." He pulled his horse around and started back. Santee sat in his saddle for a dull five minutes, not so much angry as puzzled. He knew these southwestern rivers. Sometimes they were a mile wide, and ran only a thin trickle for fifty weeks out of the year. The other two weeks they would run full to the banks. But this was not one of those rivers. This was a mountain stream, full the year round. Yesterday there had been thunderheads over the Utes, which meant that the Rio Medio should be running an especially full head of water. Something was wrong.

He thought of the legal end of it. If it could be proven in court that the old stream bed, wet or dry, was the Rio Medio, then he was safe. But what if the stream had changed its course? What if there was a Rio Medio that didn't flow through this canyon? Then he'd have to find the water that should be flowing down this canyon.

He cut back to the stream bed and started his curious journey up it. Early afternoon passed into late, and he was still following the ghost of a river. It had happened recently, this change, for the clay banks were still wet where they were shaded. He went on and on, his puzzlement growing stronger. It gave him an uneasy feeling, one that he could not satisfactorily explain. It was as if he had revisited a town he was familiar with, only to find a green prairie where the hotel had stood, and the ashes of a campfire and a rusty tomato can the only clues that there had once been a single soul there.

It was dusk and the canyon was in deep shadow when he rounded a bend where the canyon shouldered into the mountain range. He pulled up his horse with a yank that hurt its mouth and looked ahead of him.

There was wall there, a solid wall of rubble and clay and stone that cut across the breadth of the canyon and dammed it. He considered this for a full minute. Yes, it was a dam, all right, but water piles up behind a dam until it spills over. He dismounted, his face scowling, and scaled the rubble face. On top, he could see that the dam was thick. He walked the hundred feet of its loose-dirt top until he came to its other edge.

And then everything was explained. This dam was diverting the water to the right, through a raw cut in the ridge that divided the old stream bed from its new one, a canyon that angled off toward the east. Santee stood there looking at it in amazement.

"Dynamite did it, Santee," a voice drawled from behind him. Santee whirled. Sam Teacher stood on the embankment behind him. Even while he was looking, a second man climbed the embankment and stood beside Sam.

"Oh," Santee said in a weak voice.

"I just blew out the ridge into the old stream bed," Sam said. "Then I caved down this shoulder to make sure of the dam. Like it, Santee?"

Santee tried to laugh. "I can fix that, Sam. I can get dynamite, too."

Sam laughed now, clear and soft in the twilight. "There's just three reasons why you won't do that, Santee. First one is, this ain't your land. The second is, I've already warned Drury to send guards up here tonight to see you don't. The third is—you won't live to fix anything." He paused. "You're a dead man, Santee."

Santee judged the distance to Sam. It was about thirty feet. Sam didn't have a gun in his hand, and neither did his companion. But Sam could get a gun in his hand uncomfortably fast. At Santee's back was the stream. Here, crowded into this narrow canyon, it was swift and deep and boiling. All this he saw and thought of in a split second, and he felt the hair on the back of his neck rise. This was it—and he was afraid.

"Wait a minute, Sam," Santee said.

"Only till you go for your gun."

"We can—"

"Talk, sure. Only I don't want any. This was a promise, Santee. Remember? The only reason you didn't finish me when you had me there in the *rincon* was because you needed somebody to lay that murder on. I don't need you to saddle a murder on, Santee. Now cut loose your dogs, or I'll do it myself."

Santee took the only way out. He pushed himself backward toward the stream. Even as he was falling he saw Sam's hand whip down, up, and saw it explode hip-high. He felt something claw across his chest, and then he hit the water. He turned, diving, and felt his gun slip out of its holster. The water was hurling him along, and he put out his hands to keep from being dashed to pieces.

When he thought his lungs were going to burst, he came to the surface, gulped, and dived again. The current had taken him far downstream now. But he stayed under a second time and a third and fourth and fifth. When it was fully dark, miles down the stream, he pulled in to the bank and clung to a piñon branch. He was shivering now, but not with cold, for the night was warm. Sam Teacher, he knew, would be on his trail at daylight.

He pulled himself out of the stream and then examined his wound. Sam's aim, as always, had been faultless. Santee had fallen backward, and so was almost parallel with the trajectory of Sam's bullet when it hit him. It had hit his lowest rib and been deflected up through the skin of his chest. It smarted a little, but that was all. He wrung out his clothes, threw his coat and shell belt into the stream, and then crawled up the bank. He would have to travel all night, and cloud his back trail as he had never done before.

All through that night he kept on walking, working his way toward Trabajo. When the sun came up he was far west along the rim. He picked out a thick cedar, climbed into the highest branch that would hold him—which was only a few feet off the ground—and waited. He did not sleep that whole day. When darkness came again, he found a trail down the rim, and kept on to Trabajo.

At daylight he walked into the town, footsore and exhausted.

Of the clerk at the hotel desk he asked, "Is Colver gone?"

The clerk said yes and stared at Santee, who smiled bitterly, too tired to curse.

"Is your dining room open?" Santee asked.

"No, sir, won't be for an hour."

Santee dragged himself up the stairs to his room and sat on the bed. He was exhausted and wanted to sleep, but he was so hungry that his stomach, thirty-six hours without food, sawed and coiled and ached. He put on a clean shirt, washed, and went downstairs again.

"Where can I eat at this hour?" he asked.

"Well, the Gem Café is open early for the punchers."

Santee went out and turned down the side street that ran off the northwest corner of the plaza. His gaze roved the street constantly, for even if he was fairly certain that Sam Teacher wouldn't have the nerve to follow him into town, he couldn't be sure.

Only when he stepped into the empty Gem Café did he relax a little. He took a stool at the counter, and Celia Drury came up to him for his order. Without looking at her he ordered steak and coffee and pie, and when it came he wolfed it down while he waited for a second order of the same.

Celia, who by now was used to a cowpuncher's appetite, watched him covertly and with amazement. When he was finished, Santee pulled out a cigar and lighted it and only then looked at her. He had his mouth open to speak to her when his brow wrinkled and he stared.

"Haven't I seen you somewhere before, miss?" he asked.

She said, "Sure, I'm the girl of your dreams," and went on clearing away the dishes. Santee, however, did not laugh, and he kept staring at her in a way that made her uncomfortable.

"But I haven't been here before. What's your name?"

Celia turned her head and called, "Double-Jack."

Double-Jack came out of the kitchen, wiping his hands on his apron. Without having to ask any questions, he paused in front of Santee and put both hands on the counter. "Mister, she won't go out with you. She don't like jewels and she don't want to see St. Louis. Her name is Celia Drury and she don't give a damn what yours is, so pay your bill and have the kindness to peddle that whisky-drummer talk somewhere else."

Santee smiled. "Celia Drury. That's it. I wasn't talking for nothing, and I knew it. I'm Santee Bales, miss," he said to Celia. "I was your brother's partner. You look like him."

Celia said, "It's all right, Double-Jack," and Double-Jack went back into the kitchen. Celia surveyed Drury with cool curiosity.

"You're the man that helped Steve to fool Dad out of the Rio Medio canyon?"

"That's right." Santee made a shrewd guess then. "If the deal had gone through, young lady, you would have been the richer by several thousand dollars."

"But Steve's dead. You don't owe him anything."

"I know. Still, he wouldn't want it left to your dad, after the treatment he got. I was going to put his share to your account."

"I could use it." Celia laughed. "But you speak as if it's past."

Santee shrugged, and made a palms-up gesture with his hands. "Believe me, it is."

"The railroad wouldn't buy it?"

Santee told her about the Rio Medio having been shifted from its course, of his ride up the canyon to the dam, of his fight with Sam Teacher, and of his escape.

"But he can't do that!" she said.

Santee shrugged. "He did it."

"But those poor farmers below! What will they do for water?"

Santee had been staring at the tip of his cigar, rolling it in his fingers. Now his fingers ceased toying with the cigar, and he raised his head slowly, until he was staring at Celia.

"You mean there are farmers using that water for irrigation?"

"Of course. All the people below have gardens and fields. They'll be robbed of their water."

Santee dropped his cigar and smacked his fist on the counter. "That's it! That's all I need!"

He rose and hurried out. On the way to the livery stable he almost ran. In another five minutes, he was galloping out of town toward Santa Luz.

CHAPTER THIRTEEN

DOUBLE-JACK had told Celia to take Monday off, but she refused. She was trying to please him, Double-Jack knew, but still she needed fresh air and a rest. And something else, too. Along toward late afternoon, Double-Jack untied his apron and said, "I'm sick of this dump. I'm goin' for a ride. You comin'?"

"With nobody left to serve customers? Of course I'm not."

"I'm lockin' up," Double-Jack said. "It don't make no difference whether you're here or not. If you want to ride with me, come along. If you don't, then go sleep or call on your friends."

"I'd like to ride with you, Double-Jack."

When the horses came around from the livery stable, Celia said, "Where'll we go?"

"West, out in the grass. I'd like to take my boots off and wade in the stuff."

Celia smiled at him and agreed. They rode out west on the road toward the Star 22, and Celia was very quiet. Double-Jack talked incessantly and tried to make her laugh. But it was uphill work, and by dusk he gave it up.

"Hadn't we better turn back?" Celia asked, as darkness approached.

"Just a little ways more."

When they topped the low rise from which they could see the lights of the Star 22 off in the distance, Celia pulled up. "This is far enough," she said.

Double-Jack swung a leg over the saddle horn. "Not quite," he said. "Whyn't we go see Matt?"

Celia's back straightened. "I don't guess so," she said quietly and firmly.

Double-Jack scratched his head. "Hell, it's what I come for."

"Then go ahead."

"Not without you." He snorted. "Why do you think I brung you out this far, sis?"

"I'm not going to see Dad," Celia said firmly.

"Look. You got a job, ain't you? You're earnin' your livin', ain't you? You don't have to ask Matt Drury for anything, not even a kind word. All right, he's a lonesome old man. It ain't goin' to hurt you a bit to drop in and say hello to him and cheer him up. You done it for me that time I had to stay in Doc Bleeker's house with a broke leg. And I wasn't even your dad."

"You needed it."

"So does he. If you're set on bein' ornery, why, come along and crow about the job you're holdin'. I don't think you will, though. You'll likely ride in and turn down his offer to come home and tell him you got a job and ask about everything and maybe get a cup of coffee and you'll feel better and so will he—so what the hell, sis. Ain't it easy?"

Double-Jack's tone was as close to pleading as it ever got. Celia understood, too, what lay behind it. Double-Jack loved them both, and he was trying to heal a wound that her stubbornness kept open. She considered everything he had said, and found he spoke only the truth. Strangely enough, in this last week she had found that she had a new kind of pride. It was pride in work, in independence, and her father couldn't take that from her.

"All right, but I'm doing it for you, Double-Jack."

"That's more like it," Double-Jack grunted.

They rode on into the darkness and pulled up and dismounted under the old cottonwoods by the wall. Celia felt a nostalgia for the place, for its quiet beauty and peace. She fought it down as Double-Jack opened the door in the wall and they entered the patio.

There was only one lamp lighted in the house, and it was in the dining room. Through the double doors, which were open to the night, Celia could see her father at the big dining table eating alone. In spite of herself, she felt a surge of pity. He looked so lonely and so old in there.

Double-Jack coughed and led the way across the patio. Drury looked up as Double-Jack entered, and a smile started, and then he saw Celia. He rose, bewilderment and pleasure on his lean face. Some of the fire had been drained from his eyes, but he was still the same figure of power and generosity that Double-Jack had always worshiped.

"Come in, come in, both of you," Drury said. He shook Double-Jack's hand and asked after him, and only then did he turn to Celia and put out his hand. He kissed her cheek, and then gestured to the chairs and called for the maid.

Her father, Celia saw, was carrying it off the way it should be carried off, and she was grateful to him. Celia greeted the maid, whose face was flushed with pleasure at seeing her, and then Drury ordered two more places set. While Drury talked with Double-Jack and the food was brought in, Celia relaxed. With a new perception, she saw how handsome and spacious this room was—this whole life was. It had taken a job as a waitress and a musty little attic room to open her eyes to it.

When Drury had given her plenty of time, he asked quietly, "How's the job, honey?"

Celia was immediately on the defensive. But when she looked at her father she understood that he wasn't gloating. "Hard work. Good work. Good food, too."

Drury said, "She lost you any money, Double-Jack?"

"Only in countin'."

"How's that?"

Double-Jack's jaundiced old eyes lighted up with amusement, but his face was perfectly sober. "Well, whenever a check runs higher than ten dollars, she's got to take off her shoes to count."

Celia giggled, and Drury put back his head and laughed.

Suddenly his laughter ceased and he stared beyond Celia.

Celia swiveled her head to see Pearly, unshaven and dirty and smiling, standing in the doorway.

"Do I get arrested if I shake hands?" Pearly asked.

"Why, you damned old fool!" Matt exploded. "Come in!"

Pearly yanked off his hat and walked over to Matt and put out his hand. It was when he was holding Matt's hand tight in his own that Sam Teacher stepped through the door, his step slow and light and careful.

Drury saw him first and he tried to pull his gun hand out of Pearly's, but Pearly held tight.

"Easy, Matt. We got somethin' to say to you. Sit down and listen and gimme your promise you won't draw that gun."

"On the man that killed my son!" Drury blazed. "I will not!"

For answer, Pearly reached down and slipped Drury's gun from its holster, and only then released Matt's hand. Sam Teacher, his face burned to a clean brown from the weather, smiled and leaned on the doorjamb.

"You can't do nothin', Matt. Sit down," Pearly urged.

Drury sank into his chair, his eyes wicked with anger. Celia was watching Sam Teacher, noting how casual he was. Then her glance shifted to Pearly, searching for guilt and shame in his face. All she saw was the same old seamed face hidden behind the handful of hay he called a mustache. It looked a little less worried, a little more friendly, if anything. When she felt Sam's cold stare, she dropped her glance to her plate. Double-Jack, too old a hand for excitement like this, grinned at Pearly and was quiet.

"Thrown in with the killer, have you, Pearly?" Drury asked hotly. "I'd never have believed it!"

Pearly nodded indifferently. "We don't want you to talk, Matt. We just want you to listen. It's for your own good."

With an effort of will, Drury composed his face and

inclined his head. His eyes were wary.

Sam Teacher strolled into the room then and half-sat on the table and leaned forward, almost in front of Celia. "Drury," he said, "the Rio Medio ain't where it was a couple of days ago. Pearly and me have diverted it into another canyon. It flows off the rim about ten miles east of where it used to come down. If you're a wise man, you'll keep it there."

"What are you talking about?" Drury asked curtly.

"Santee Bales come out with the Southwestern and Rio Grande agent Saturday to sell that strip of land you deeded to Steve." He explained to Drury how the grant boundary was the river, not the canyon, and how by shifting the river they had prevented Santee from selling the piece.

"But unless you keep that piece of land guarded until Bales is killed, you're goin' to lose it again."

"Until Bales is killed?" Drury echoed. "Who's going to kill him?"

"I am."

Drury stared at him. "You mean you're going to set out after a man and hunt him down and kill him in cold blood?"

"It ain't cold," Sam said. "Whenever I think of him, it ain't cold."

Celia said in quiet anger, "You almost succeeded two nights ago, didn't you?"

Sam's glance swiveled to her. "That's right. That was my hard luck."

Drury put both hands on the table and rose. "Let me get this straight. You want my men to guard this make-shift dam of yours while you go out and kill Bales?"

"You want the railroad to come through Rio Medio canyon?" Sam countered.

"I don't want the railroad anywhere near me!" Drury flared. "But if I'm supposed to tolerate murder to keep it out, then I'll let it be built through this house if need be!"

"Santee Bales killed Steve, Matt," Pearly said quietly.

Drury pointed a finger at Sam. "That gunman killed Steve! Think of that while you're riding with him!"

Sam lounged off the table. "You won't put a guard up there until you hear Bales is dead?"

"No."

Sam looked at Pearly. "All right, Pearly." To Drury he said, "Maybe you won't have to, at that. Because I'm goin' to kill Bales whether you do it or not."

"I won't have anything to do with murder," Drury said firmly.

Sam turned to go, and Celia rose out of her chair. "Wait," she said.

Sam paused in the door. "The last time you said that to me and I didn't do it, I got cuffed. You aim to cuff me again?"

"Please," Celia said patiently. "Step outside with me."

She went out into the dark patio and Sam followed her. "I–I'd like to straighten all this out in my mind," she said in a low voice. "Will you answer my questions?"

"Any."

"Remember, too, that even if Steve Drury was my brother, I didn't love him. He didn't deserve to be murdered, but he didn't deserve any medals, either."

"All right."

"Did Santee Bales kill Steve?"

"You heard Pearly say it."

"For that piece of land that the railroad wants as a right-of-way?"

"That's right."

"And you saved the right-of-way for Dad by diverting the Rio Medio?"

"Yes."

She was quiet a long time, thinking this over. "Why?" she asked then.

"Somebody's got to fight for him," Sam pointed out. "He won't fight for himself." He paused. "No, that's not it, either. I've fought Bales for five years. It's a private thing–a feud between him and me."

"Then the right-of-way is only incidental?"

Sam didn't answer for a long moment, then he said, "I only want to keep Santee from gettin' it."

"But he will," Celia said.

"Not if he's dead."

"But he's not here. He's gone." She told him of her conversation of the morning. "When I mentioned that about the irrigation, he dropped his cigar, slammed his hand on the counter, and said, 'That's it. That's all I need.' " She paused. "Don't you see? It means—"

"Sure I see," Sam said quietly. "It means he'll get a writ from a judge makin' us put the Rio Medio back where it was."

"And it will be enforced, too."

Sam only nodded.

"And that means that Dad will lose that piece of land, after all."

Sam sighed. "It looks that way. I can't catch Santee when he's got a day's start on me. And when he gets to a judge, it's done."

Celia was quiet.

Sam said curiously, "It sounds like you want your dad to have that land. Why?"

"Oh, I don't know," Celia said in a low voice.

"When I last saw you, you'd have throwed in with Bales to get it, if it would hurt your Dad. Now you've changed your mind."

"But Dad's honest!"

"Sure. He always has been. You just findin' it out?"

"No, it isn't that," Celia said quietly. "It's—well, I've deserted him. Pearly's left him. Steve's gone. He's alone now, and he can't fight trouble the way he used to. I just saw it tonight." She looked at Sam in the dark. "You and Pearly are really trying to help him. And you're the only ones."

Sam laughed bitterly. "He won't let us."

Celia put her hand on his arm. "Help him, won't you? I can't."

"How?" Sam asked gently.

"I don't know. There must be a way. If there is, you can find it."

Sam said, "That's a funny thing for you to be sayin'."

Celia nodded agreement. "When I left here I hated him for trying to break me. I hated you for saying the things you did. But I've learned several things since I've been working. One of them is that Dad was right in trying to break me. Another is that I'm happier at work than I've ever been in my life. And the third is—is that if Pearly was willing to quit his job to break you out of jail, then you can't be as bad as I thought. And now you're trying to help Dad—and I am, too. Only, I can't, and you can—if there is anybody that can."

As if she had said too much, she left him then and went back into the house. In a moment, Pearly stepped out to join Sam and they vanished into the night.

Drury sat staring at his plate, anger giving way to bewilderment in his face. Finally he looked up at Celia, as if asking for help. Celia smiled gently at him. "You do what you think is right, Dad. Only, Pearly is trying to help you. You know that."

"But—murder."

"Of a killer."

"Of a man by a killer," Drury said quietly. "No, railroad or no railroad, I won't share in that."

CHAPTER FOURTEEN

TWENTY MILES to the east of Trabajo and far up in the Utes was the Giant Glorieta mine. Nestled in the high timber, its shaft house, candle house, office, and barns were just as gray and weathered as the slab shacks housing the miners and their families. Five years of almost daily rain or snow had grayed their lumber to the color of the boulder fields higher on the peak. It was a tight little community, for Sand Forks, where the reduction mills were, lay some thirty miles away. The log saloon and store in Glorieta supplied some cheer for the camp, but the men who drove the freight wagons loaded with ore down to Sand Forks were looked upon with envy: twice each week they escaped the rainy monotony of the camp in summer, and its bitter cold in winter.

George Harnum was such a man. Mondays and Thursdays each week he would mount the seat of the big high-wheeled ore freighter which stood under the tipple, pick up the jerkline and his whip, and with bull-throated shouts and curses get his five teams of mules into movement. It would always be early in the morning, and Harnum would be bundled up in a mackinaw and heavy boots and, if it was raining, as it was on this morning, in a long yellow slicker.

The toughest part of the trip was getting cold mules to pull over the hump of the ridge that lay just beyond the camp. After that, it was downhill all the way, and a man only had to understand a mule's mind and the braking of an ore wagon to make it a pleasant trip. It did get a bit lonesome with nothing but dripping timber and steaming mules as companions, although occasionally, when you had to pass an up-wagon on an especially narrow part of the rocky road, it could be exciting. But usually it was a little lonesome.

It was with considerable interest, therefore, that George, an hour out of camp, beheld a slickered man standing beside the road holding the reins of a horse. When the wagon was almost abreast of him, the man raised a hand to indicate that he wanted to speak with George. With considerable ease George pulled his teams up and, foot on the brake, said, "Howdy."

"Howdy. I lamed my horse. Any chance of catchin' a lift down to the Forks?"

George spat over the side and regarded him. He was a runt, nothing more than a kid in appearance, but he could talk and that was all George wanted. "Plenty. Tie him to the end-gate and climb up."

The other did so, and George whipped the mules into motion again.

"I never rode on these-here things before," the runt said, examining the wagon and its load. "What is it?"

"Ore. Ain't you never seen ore before?"

George's passenger, blue-eyed and innocent, shook his head in negation. "Not me. All I ever see is cows." He peered under the tarp at the load of grayish-looking rock and said, "Don't tell me that damn stuff is worth haulin' down to the Forks."

George laughed indulgently. "Mister, you're ridin' on about three thousand dollars worth of gold. That's high-grade stuff."

The cowboy looked properly awed, and George went on to explain the process of reduction. The cowboy gave him a smoke and listened. He asked questions about the mule-skinning job, and George warmed up to him. "There ain't nothin' to it," George said. "You drive the lead team with this jerkline. The rest of them jacks you beat into line and keep 'em from straddlin' that chain."

The cowboy nodded. "There's a lot of pull there, all

right. Could you take off acrost country with this rig and get anywheres?"

"If it was reasonable flat," George said, "I could go anywheres."

The cowboy reached under his slicker, as if to get a match, and when his hand came out it held a gun, which he pointed at George.

"Well, I reckon that's what you're goin' to have to do," he said quietly.

George glanced down at the gun, then at the man holding it, and licked his lips. "Listen, cowboy. You aim to steal this ore?"

"That's right."

"What good's it gunna do you? You can't buy whisky with rock."

"Ever tried?"

That one stumped George. He thought awhile, then glanced obliquely at the other's face and saw the mocking light in the eyes, and grinned sheepishly.

"You can't ride me, cowboy. No, I ain't ever tried, but I know it ain't so."

"I'm goin' to try it," came the grave statement. "You just drive this up to the saloon I name, and I'll bet I can stay drunk for three weeks."

George looked at him again, and decided he was loco. They drove on for a while in silence, and then George said, "You better put that iron away. I'm due to meet another wagon pretty quick."

"That's what you think."

"I know."

"No, you don't. You're goin' to take the right-hand road when we come to the fork down here."

George's forehead wrinkled. He was trying to think of any fork. and then he remembered the old wagon trail that had been abandoned years ago because of its grade. It was weed-grown and steep, and a man had to look carefully to see that it had ever existed.

George exploded. "Why, dammit, man. You loco? They

give that road up because it was so steep! It's all washed out!"

"No, it ain't. I come over it."

"But I can't drive that!"

"You just been tellin' me how good you was, and how easy it is to handle this rig," the other said innocently. There was an undertone of jeering, however, that George did not like.

"All right. Suppose I can. Where you goin' when you take the road? It levels off at the flat, then heads for the rim, then it follows the rim west for ten miles or so and peters out. The place where you used to could get down off the rim has washed out. There ain't any road."

"That's right."

"All right. Where you goin'?"

"To the rim."

George was filled with despair. "Look, I'll lose my job over this."

"Why?"

"Why, dammit, this ore is worth three thousand dollars! And these mules and this wagon! I s'pose you're goin' to take them, too."

"I'll pay for it."

George looked at him. "Sure. In what? Beercaps?"

Sam Teacher pulled off a boot with his free hand, and pulled out a sheaf of dirty bills. He peeled off three of them, put the others back in the boot, and put it on. "Here's three thousand," he told George, handing him the money. "I ain't goin' to keep the wagon and mules, so I won't pay for them."

George gulped in amazement, just as Sam said, "Here's the fork."

George pulled up and regarded the cutoff. While he was looking a second man in a slicker stepped out from behind a tree, a shovel in his hands. He was an old-timer with a ragged mustache, and he leaned against the tree without saying a word. George looked from him to the small man on the seat.

"All right. There's the road," Sam said.

"You goin' through with this?" George asked desperately.

"Not me. You are. You're goin' to drive this load of ore where I tell you to, and earn fifty dollars. I give you the money for the ore, so no harm's done except you had a change of scenery. What's the matter with that?"

George looked earnestly at him, and saw no weakening in the face. Then he looked at the gun and decided it meant business. He looked at the road, and it challenged him. He was single, strong, and could get a job anywhere in case he was fired over this. So he picked up the jerkline, rose out of his seat, and braced his feet. "Be damned to you," he said. "I can drive that old road wet or dry. Hang on."

He cursed the mules and shook out his whip, popping it with a crack that made the timber ring. The mules, once they knew that a change had come over their lives, lunged into their collars.

The wagon lurched off the road, hung on two wheels, righted itself, and plunged on. The old road was grown over with second-growth pines that scraped the mules' bellies and tickled them. George sat down, put a foot on the brake, and let them have their head. Sam glanced back once, in time to see Pearly filling in the wagon tracks and smoothing them over. With a few hours of this rain, which would blot out even the tracks on the road, it would take some careful observing to see where the wagon had left the road.

And then Sam turned his attention to the ride. Ascending the road, it had looked steep, but not too steep. Now it looked like a precipice. As the wagon gained way and the mules stretched out, Sam had a hard time remembering that he was supposed to be holding a gun on the driver. His first impulse was to jump, his second to drop the gun and hold on with both hands. But George sat there with a grim smile on his face, the smile of a man who is taking a dare and will see it through to the bitter end. Sam took a deep breath, decided not to look at the road, and held his gun pointed at George's belly.

The only thing slow about that ride was the passage of time. Twice Sam got ready to jump as the heavy wagon careened on two wheels. Once, George lunged to his feet and braced himself like a sailor on the slanting deck of a ship. His jaw sagged open and his jerkline slacked. They passed a tree, and the rear hub chewed bark with a rending sound. It came so close that the lead horse shied away. And then the wagon settled down again with a crash, and George's whip cracked out. The mules leaned into the collars on a small upgrade, and Sam breathed freely again.

After that they were leveling off for the flats. When they finally pulled clear of the timber and then the foothills, George pulled the teams up to blow them. He glanced at Sam with a triumphant expression and wiped the rain from his face. "Wasn't so bad," he drawled, but there was a queer pitch to his voice that told Sam they had been lucky to get through.

Pearly caught up with them at noon when they were several miles along the rim. The going was easy here in spite of the mud, for a few inches under its surface was the cap rock of the rim.

In midafternoon they came to the new Rio Medio. It had spread out now so that it was only a shallow stream whose banks were not yet wholly defined. A quarter-mile to the south of the road it tumbled off the rim. The wind caught it then, whipping it out in long streamers and splashing it onto the plains below in ragged banners. Farther on, it collected in a small lake and spilled out from it in a meandering stream that headed roughly southeast.

They camped that night after dark in a clump of cedars near the rim where Pearly had cached grain for the mules and food for themselves. George, now that he had got used to the idea of the ore wagon being stolen, was amiable enough. It was a wet, raw night, with the rain whipping in under the tarp they had rigged up for a shelter, and they were glad to climb into dry blankets after they ate.

Pearly, a light sleeper, slept on the guns in case George decided to make a break, but George did not stir.

The rain still held on the next morning, and for a reason George could not explain, this fact seemed to make both his captors happy. They helped him harness the teams, and an hour after daylight they were on their way again—where to, George had given up even trying to guess. In midmorning Sam gave orders to leave the road and work toward the foothills, and a little after noon they came to the junction of the foothills and the empty canyon bed of the old Rio Medio.

George looked down into the canyon and shook his head. "This is as far as we go, mister," he announced.

"Can you get down into the canyon?"

George nodded gravely. "Sure. Only we're goin' to stay there once we're down. I can take this damn thing down anything. It's gettin' up that can't be done."

"All right. Put it down in the stream bed."

George, who had already resigned himself to this idiocy, shrugged and dismounted to rig up a roughlock with a log and chain. Once it was adjusted, he whipped the mules over the sloping rim and the ponderous wagon slid down into the canyon. George looked at the stream, which was flowing a couple of inches of water on its shallow bed, looked at the opposite canyon wall, and put down the jerkline. "All right," he said, "now what you goin' to do? Rustle up another dozen mules?"

"Turn downstream," Sam called from the slope.

George did as he was bid and then stopped while Sam came over to him. "I want you to drive real slow down this stream bed. You got that? Real slow. Wait till I give you the word to start."

Pearly joined him, carrying two shovels, and they both climbed up on the load and removed the tarp.

"All right," Sam said.

George got the mules in motion, and then turned around to observe Sam and Pearly. They were leisurely shoveling out ore into the stream bed and scattering it in a wide arc. George watched them for many long minutes, paying more attention to them than to the mules, who were splashing water shoulder high.

Finally, when George could stand it no longer, he pulled up the mules. Gravely, as if talking to children, he said, "Look. Didn't nobody ever tell you that you can't plant that stuff? Ore don't grow into gold watches if it's watered. Ain't nobody ever told you that?"

Sam looked at Pearly and they both laughed. Sam said, "Turn around and keep those mules movin'. Drive right on down this canyon until you're free of it."

Santee Bales arrived late at night in Trabajo and went immediately to the sheriff's office on the chance that Lovejoy might be there. But the office was dark, and he went back to the hotel, every restless move proclaiming his impatience.

He was waiting on the doorstep of the sheriff's office the next morning, his face bland and important-looking. Against the heat of the morning, which had come on the heels of the long rain, Santee was wearing a black broadcloth coat.

He flourished a paper in Lovejoy's face and said, "Sheriff, prepare for a shock."

"They ain't caught Teacher, have they?" Lovejoy asked.

Santee laughed. "Oh, no, nothing like that. But Teacher doesn't matter any more. This paper is a writ from the court in Santa Luz. It's an order restraining anyone from diverting the water of the Rio Medio from its course."

"Unh-hunh," Lovejoy said.

"And this," Santee added, bringing out an envelope, "is a court order directing you to divert the Rio Medio back into its rightful channel."

Lovejoy read this too. "All right," he said. "Only how'm I goin' to do it?"

"Dynamite. Blow out that dam."

"Who foots the bill for it?"

"The Inter-Valley Irrigation Company."

"And who is that?"

"Me. I incorporated a few of those Mexican farmers down south of here into a company, hired a lawyer in Santa Luz, got an injunction and a court order, and promised to pay the bill for diverting the water back into its rightful channel. Now get a crew together—say ten men—order your dynamite, hire a dozen pack horses for the tools, and let's get busy."

Lovejoy scratched his head. "Well, it's legal enough, all right."

By midmorning Sheriff Lovejoy had rousted out a crew of workmen. He chose only those men who had had experience in blasting—prospectors and miners. He explained the job to them, then hired the pack horses, collected tools and dynamite, and set out. Santee rode across the bridge at the head of his workmen. In Santa Luz he had succeeded in finding Ross Colver, who was waiting out the time limit of two more weeks that had been set for securing the right-of-way. Colver was on his way up here now, and when he arrived he would find the Rio Medio back where it belonged. Surveyors were coming with him to stake out the boundaries, and the legal end of it was already in the hands of the company lawyers, who were only waiting Colver's final word.

They arrived at the canyon after midday and Santee explained the diversion to the interested sheriff, who had not bothered to come out and see it before.

As they progressed up the canyon, Santee noticed that some of his men were dropping behind. Once he turned in the saddle to see two of them dismounted in the dry stream bed. They seemed to be examining something. Santee rode on ahead, but when, fifteen minutes later, his men were not in sight, he halted Lovejoy and they turned back.

The ten workmen, all dismounted, were picking up rocks from the bed of the stream.

Santee rode in among them and said, "What's the trouble here?" in a voice that was firm with authority.

The nearest man came over to him and shoved a rock at him. "Look at that, mister."

Santee looked. "What is it?"

The others were gathered about him now. Three or four of the men, prospectors, said in chorus, "Gold-bearing ore."

Santee handed the rock back. "Interesting," he commented. "Let's be on our way, though."

"You ain't gettin' me on my way," one man said. "I've quit. I'm goin' to look around here for about two hours, then ride back and stake out my claim."

"Where?" Santee asked.

"Right where you're standin', maybe."

Santee laughed. "That would be foolish. In a day or so the place where I'm standing will be running four feet of water from bank to bank."

The men looked at each other and one man spoke up. "Maybe you don't savvy what this means, Bales. There's gold here. *Gold!* The whole damn river bed! It's worth a hell of a lot more than havin' water here!"

Santee stared at them. "The court says to put this river back in its course. And it's going back."

One of the workmen, a husky prospector, came up to Santee and put a hand on his horse's neck. "Now that's where you're wrong. I wouldn't want to say for certain, but this looks like a strike, and a good strike. And nobody's goin' to turn a river onto the claim I stake out."

Santee turned to Lovejoy. "Sheriff, what are your orders?"

Lovejoy was an old-timer; all his life he had lived in a country where the raggedest prospector might turn into a rich man inside a month. He said, "Let me see that ore!"

Santee reached out and knocked the ore out of the hand of the man who was offering it to Lovejoy. "That's not the question!" he said sharply. "You've got a court order. You're bound to carry it out."

"Don't be a damn fool, sheriff," one of the men said. "We got a strike here. Stake out a claim and you'll be a rich man. You goin' to let that loudmouth talk you out of a fortune?"

"He's got a court order."

"They come a dollar a dozen," the husky prospector sneered. "Hell, give me a day and I'll get you five that'll tell you to keep the river out of this canyon."

"This is my land!" Bales shouted.

"Now is it?" the husky prospector mocked. "Accordin' to the story goin' the rounds, it ain't your land until you get the river moved back here. Your land goes three miles west of the Rio Medio and this ain't the Rio Medio—yet."

"It's Drury's, then. He'll kick you off it when he finds there's gold here. You won't get a pokeful of dust out of it!"

The prospector snorted. "Since when does a man own a watercourse? Hell, they're public domain. Else how do you figure these Mex hoe-men to the south can use this water?"

Santee made his first mistake. He said, "Do whatever you want. I'll go back to town and get a crew that will do this job for me."

The prospector turned to his mates. "Hear that?"

They crowded up to Santee, their faces threatening.

"You ain't goin' anywhere," one of them said.

Santee made his second mistake. He tried to yank his horse into a rear. The husky prospector grabbed the bridle and held the horse down. A second and third reached up and yanked Santee out of the saddle and threw him on the ground.

"Wait a minute, now," the husky prospector said. "We got to work this careful. Let me talk a minute."

At their nods he went on, Lovejoy listening attentively. "This tinhorn has got a court order. All right, all we need is a few days to hunt up a judge and get another court order. Now it don't matter who's right in this business, because we'll hire lawyers and he'll hire lawyers and it'll take two months of lawin' to get a decision. By that time we'll have a fortune, all of us, out of this ore. All right, here's what we ought to do. We'll hold this jughead until we can get Lovejoy a court order restrainin' Bales. Today we'll go up and down the creek putting up our monuments. Tonight we'll register our claims. Me, I'll ride for the court order. Joe will file my claim. After we got 'em all filed, then we'll turn the town loose here." He laughed. "Hell, if they turn that river on a couple of hundred claims, we'll law 'em till we're gray!"

The men yelled assent, excitement in their eyes. The spokesman turned to Lovejoy. "You with us or agin' us, sheriff?"

Lovejoy looked surprised. He said, "Well, I—"

"You're with us," one man shouted. "You damn well better be. We elected you."

"Can't you arrest this Bales on a charge of disturbin' the peace till Mel gets back with the court order?"

"I could," Lovejoy admitted.

"You will. Now git off your horse and start hunting your location, sheriff."

Sheriff Lovejoy, avoiding Santee's eyes, dismounted, the fever beginning to stir him. Santee cursed him with savage bitterness. He offered bribes, he threatened, he cajoled, but he was talking to men already drunk with riches. They appointed a couple of men to guard him while they staked their claims up and down the creek and put up their monuments. Only darkness stopped them.

Then came the race for town. The dynamite and tools were forgotten. Santee, tied in his saddle, was put in front so they would not lose him, and then the stampede began. It was a wild ride; these men were willing to kill their horses if they could get to a brother or friend in time so that he, too, could stake out a claim.

In town, Santee was hustled into the jail, chained in the one empty cell with a padlock, and then forgotten. In the fifteen minutes after the news broke, every house in town was lighted up. Horses were at a premium. Rich gold-bearing ore had been found in the bed of the Rio Medio!

From his window in the jail, Santee saw it all happen, and he could have wept. Spring wagons, buckboards, hayricks, saddle horses, mules, burros, anything that could carry a man, milled about the plaza and poured out the east road over the bridge. Men were shooting in the air, giving the long yell that raised a man's hackles with excitement. Even the womenfolk joined in. A fortune, ease and security and riches for the rest of their lives, lay within striking distance. Dignity could be forgotten for the moment in the face of that. There were fights in the plaza. Wagons tangled and were upset. Disorder was everywhere, and Lovejoy did not make any attempt to stop it. Trabajo had the gold fever. And Trabajo, Santee thought bitterly, had the Rio Medio canyon. By daylight, its sides would be blanketed with claims. To move that horde of gold-seekers out would take years and a fortune. With success in his grasp, his chances had been wiped out so utterly and completely that he began to wonder if they had ever existed.

He sat on his cot and cursed until he was hoarse, and then cursed in whispers while the din of the town rose to the stars—which, after all, were only diamonds and far away, while gold was almost underfoot.

CHAPTER FIFTEEN

SAM AND PEARLY had watched that first night's stampede with amazement. What they had hoped would turn into a claim fight or two which might entangle Santee in a court delay that would halt the railroad's purchase had turned into a stampede. During the night the whole town of Trabajo moved to the old Rio Medio canyon. Lanterns, kerosene flares, and lamps weaved up and down the canyon as people hunted for room to stake claims.

The wisest of the stampeders, not finding the gold-bearing ore above and below a certain point, were convinced that the river had cut through a pocket. They began staking the sides of the canyon. The less knowing, always willing to follow those who showed some knowledge, followed suit. By morning, every inch of the canyon for ten miles was staked out, and some of the claims even ranged out onto the shelf above the rim.

By midday, the more businesslike began to straggle in with food and tarpaulins and tools and lumber. All through the next night the activity continued. Some of the men were working their claims. Others, not wholly convinced that the restraining order would be forthcoming, threw in to build a community dike which would divert the water away from their claims. Still others, going at it in a businesslike way, began on their crude shacks and tents. Canvas stores, doling out supplies at a premium which nobody could yet afford but which they were sure they eventually could, did a big business. Here was the beginning of a boom town—started by a single load of ore.

When night fell, Sam and Pearly became bold enough

to walk up to the edge of the canyon and watch the activity.

"Well, I'll be damned," Pearly kept muttering over and over. "Well, I will be damned."

Sam, however, was uneasy. What had happened to Santee? He hadn't showed up yet at the canyon. Neither had Sheriff Lovejoy, who would administer the law in this new community. Moreover, if Santee showed up with a court order, it would be Sheriff Lovejoy's job to carry it out. This started a train of thought in Sam's mind that he could not discard.

Looking down on the busy camp, Sam said, "Santee ain't showed up yet."

"He will," Pearly said. He looked over at Sam. "You aim to do what you said?"

"Kill him? I do."

"But he'll be careful enough not to travel alone, Sam. You told him you'd gun him."

Pearly had arrived at the same conclusion Sam had, but Sam elaborated. "That's right. He'll blow in with the order, hunt up Lovejoy, and then the fun will begin." He looked over at Pearly. "What if Lovejoy is locked in jail again? It'll take three days to get him out. In that time, Santee is bound to be alone sometime. He's bound to forget me for a while, ain't he?"

"What of it?"

Sam stood up and brushed his clothes off. "Nothin'. Only I'm goin' to be where I can watch him."

Pearly stood up, alarm in his every movement. "You ain't goin' to town!"

"That's it. If he just slips once, that's all I need."

Pearly argued and pleaded and begged, but Sam only laughed.

"You mean you're goin' in that jail again and throw Lovejoy in a cell?"

Sam patted the two sets of keys in his pocket. "I did it before. There ain't ten men in the town now. All I got to do is wait till Lovejoy goes into his office, then throw him in and wait for Santee to show up."

Pearly sighed, and then swore, but he knew it was useless to argue. His younger partner had a way with him that was ruthless and direct and to the point. Pearly, who had lived alongside of Anse Lovejoy for ten years, had little respect for him, yet he would have hesitated to go a third time to lock him in a cell simply because the sheriff had been doing his duty. Yet Sam did not hesitate. Neither did Sam pause at the thought of crowding a man into a gun fight. Furthermore, he not only announced his intention of getting in a gun fight, he told his opponent, the law, and anybody else who cared to listen. It was living a little too fast for Pearly's peace of mind.

He followed Sam to their horses without another word, and they mounted and rode off toward Trabajo. Presently Pearly said, "Where you aim to hide, Sam?"

"I hadn't thought of it," Sam said lightly.

Pearly said with reluctance, "Celia would hide you."

"Hunh-uh."

"It's part her fight. She'd do it, too. She's changed."

"Let's keep her out of it," Sam said quietly. "I didn't start after Santee because he'd done anything to her. Not even because he killed Steve. I'm out for him because almost since I can remember I knew the shoot-out was comin'. All I needed was the excuse. I got it now, and it don't concern her. No."

Pearly subsided, and talked of it no more, but it stuck in his mind. As they had done the time before, they paused at the bridgehead below Trabajo hours later.

"This is a one-man job," Sam said. "You can watch it, Pearly, but you ain't in it."

"But you ain't—"

"No," Sam said.

Pearly said bitterly, in a low voice, "I throwed in with you because I wanted to get Steve's killer. If Bales ain't Steve's killer, who is?"

Sam said patiently, "My promise to Santee was made long before I knew you, Pearly. I aim to keep it. Man against man, one gun each, and one of us in the dust when it ends. No, I'm doin' this alone."

"All right. Still, I'm goin' to ride in and see it."

They parted at the alley Sam had traveled up before. Pearly took to the alley, and Sam knew he was going to see Celia. He knew, too, that if he needed help, Pearly would give it to him. Only he wouldn't need help.

With one glance at the plaza, a long one which noted that the lamp in the sheriff's office was lighted, he knew what he was going to do. The plaza was practically deserted, and while it was late and some of the stores were naturally dark, the hour did not account for the look of desertion. The whole town was at the Rio Medio canyon.

He rode straight into the plaza at an easy jog, turned to the left, waved to a stranger, and pulled up in front of the sheriff's office. He even took the time to tie his pony's reins to the tie rail. He swung under it, took the three steps across the boardwalk, and opened the door to the sheriff's office.

Sheriff Lovejoy, his spectacles riding his thin nose, was poring over something at the desk while Harvey Miles stood looking over his shoulder. At the sound of the door opening, Miles turned.

He saw an undersized man, with a wicked grin on his face, holding a gun too big to fit his small hand, and that gun was pointed at him. Since Miles knew the face above that gun, he put a hand on Lovejoy's shoulder and said, "Uh—Anse."

Anse Lovejoy turned around. When he saw Sam all the life seemed to sag out of him. He took off his glasses and said with bitter resignation, "This is the last damn time I set foot in this office while I'm alive."

"You know what I want, don't you?" Sam drawled.

"Hell, yes. I ain't even goin' to argue. Come on." He stood up, ready.

Sam's glance shuttled to Miles, whose florid face had suddenly turned pale. "You was in that loud-talking posse both times, wasn't you? You was the one that started throwin' lead at me in the store that night, wasn't you?" His voice was mild.

"I never—"

"Quit it, Harvey. You'll come along," Anse said shortly.

"And cool off," Sam said. "Your blood's too hot. All right, pick up the lamp and walk in, boys."

The corridor door was already half open, and Anse Lovejoy picked up the lamp and kicked the door open the rest of the way. Sam looked about the cell block. The end cell where he had locked Lovejoy before had its bars sawed in two and bent outward and downward. He smiled at the sight of it, knowing now that he had the only set of keys. There was a man huddled in that cell, his face to the wall, a long chain padlocked to the bars and to the prisoner's leg irons.

Lovejoy said bitterly, "We ain't even got a place to lock the prisoners now."

"Take the cell on the other side," Sam said. "Nothin' like monotony to kill all the fun."

He swung wide of the sheriff, then reached in his pocket and handed him the keys. "You open it," he said.

Lovejoy opened the door and entered, and Harvey Miles entered behind him. Sam swung the door shut, then backed off to regard them.

"Well, the third time is—"

He got no further than that. A pair of strong arms grabbed him from behind, hauled him crashing back against the cell bars, and forced his arms down. He shot once into the floor, struggling in helpless fury, before a voice bawled from behind him, "Get his gun, you damned fool!"

It was Santee Bales's voice.

Lovejoy exploded out of the unlocked door. He was swinging as he ran, and the blow that Sam could not dodge caught him flush on the shelf of the chin. The darkness exploded in mounting pinwheels.

When he came to, he was roped to a cot, and leg-ironed. The lamp was on the floor, and standing in a loose circle about him were Lovejoy, Miles, and the two deputies. Old Anse Lovejoy's face reflected quiet triumph.

"Made your brag once too often, didn't you?"

"Looks that way," Sam conceded.

"Well, you don't get another chance for a break. To-night we're sending you to Santa Luz on a guarded stage. The Commissioner can worry about you from now on."

Sam's heart sank. That would be the end. As long as he was free to move in this chess game with Santee, then there was hope. But once the Commissioner got him, there was no hope at all.

"Just in case you're wonderin'," Lovejoy said, "that extry set of keys has been took out of your pocket. Also, that hole has been filled up and there's a man waitin' for Pearly in the saddle shop, just in case he reckons he can try it again."

"Go away," Sam said.

"Sure. Sure." Lovejoy grinned and motioned the others out. Before he left he untied the rope from Sam's middle, allowing him to get off the cot. The first thing Sam saw when he was sitting upright was Santee Bales in the cell across from him. Santee, hands on the bars like a caged gorilla, was laughing softly.

Memory jogged Sam. "It was you that nabbed me, eh?"

"Your old friend," Santee said. "You've been fooling around with these tank-town laws so long you forgot how to be careful."

"I ain't forgot one thing," Sam said carefully. "I can still handle a gun."

"Providing you got one. Where is it now?"

Sam's anger was pushing him, and he knew that was what Santee wanted.

"I ain't dead yet."

"Not—quite—yet," Santee said distinctly. His keen eyes searched Sam's face for any sign of fear, and there was none. Santee went on, as if musing: "Just to think, I'm getting paid five thousand dollars reward money for capturing you. And I'm going to see you hung."

Sam said gently, "But you ain't gettin' any seventy-five thousand for the right-of-way, are you, Santee?"

Santee's face clouded and he started to curse. Sam laughed, and Santee, furious now, lost his temper. With only six feet of space between them, they both stood at the bars facing each other, Sam taunting and jeering, Santee reviling Sam with a steady stream of invective.

Lovejoy found them that way when he entered a minute later and walked up to Santee's cell.

"Well, if you got the money for a twenty-five-dollar fine, you're free, Bales."

"Did you pirates get a restraining order?" Santee sneered.

"We did. You ain't goin' to move that river now, not till you fight it out in court. And just to make sure, we got a guard up there at that dam. No, sir, you're licked, Bales, and by sharper men than you are."

Lovejoy stepped through the bent bars and freed Santee. Bales came out and paused in front of Sam's cell. These two studied each other a long moment, and then Santee shrugged his wide shoulders. "It's a pity you won't live to see me get that right-of-way, Sam."

"Oh, so you're goin' to get it?" Sam asked.

Santee nodded confidently. "I don't know how, but I will. That gold strike was just plain bad luck. But Colver, the Southwestern and Rio Grande agent, is here two more weeks, cash in his pocket. I'll swing it in that time, Sam."

"Sure."

"I'll lick that gold strike. And when I do, you won't be around here to fight me."

"Don't be too sure."

Santee put out his hand, his face grave and his eyes jeering. "Well, I never like to see a man die hating me. Let's shake—before you're hung."

Sam looked at Santee's hand and then put his own through the bars to take it. Once he had hold of it, he pulled Santee toward him. Then, his feet braced against the cell bars, Santee's arm out straight and his face close,

Sam looped over a blow that caught Santee on the nose. He let go then and stepped back as Santee, his face dark with fury, tried to get at him.

"Your nose is bleedin', Santee," Sam said.

Lovejoy said, "You get out of here, Bales!"

Santee said, "I'll be there to see you hang if I have to ride a thousand miles! You'll see me, too!"

"Wipe your nose," Sam said.

Sam turned back to the cot and sat down. Evidently Santee didn't yet suspect that the ore planted in the Rio Medio canyon was Sam's work. Once he found out, of course, all he would have to do would be to get George Harnum to tell the camp how a wagonload of ore was scattered down the stream bed. The boom would collapse then, and with nobody to contest the diversion of the Rio Medio back to its original course, Santee's court order would be carried out and the right-of-way would be sold.

Sam looked about him in helpless despair. Pearly could not get him out of this. He wished he could see Pearly, could tell him what had happened, and direct him in a last move against Santee. But even that consolation would not be allowed him. He was going to a tight jail, to a trial, and to a hanging.

A murmur of conversation out in the sheriff's office came to him, and he lay down on the cot. Suddenly the corridor door opened and he turned his head. Celia was standing there, Anse Lovejoy at her side.

"So that's Steve's killer?" Celia asked in a cold voice, looking at Sam.

Sam sat up, saying nothing, as Anse, pride in his voice, said, "That's him. Bales caught him mighty pretty."

"I've never seen a killer that I was sure was a killer. May I have a look at him?"

"Go right up and look," Anse invited.

Celia came up to the bars and faced Sam. He caught her slow wink. He said insolently, "Do I look any different than I did when I worked out at the Star Twenty-Two?"

"Yes," Celia said quietly. "In my eyes you do. You look

a lot different—like a condemned man."

Sam, taking his cue, said sharply, "Don't say that! It's bad luck."

"Your conscience troubles you, doesn't it?"

Sam stared at the floor and said nothing. Celia turned to Lovejoy. "I'd like to talk to him alone. Maybe I can find out how my brother died."

Lovejoy, amazed to see Sam's defiance melting when he was faced with the sister of the man he had killed, nodded abruptly. Maybe the girl could get a confession out of him. He backed out, saying, "Be very careful, Miss Drury. He's dangerous."

When the door was closed, Celia said, "Oh, Sam, why didn't you come to the café before you tried it? I could have told you Santee was in there!"

"I should have," Sam said ruefully.

Celia turned around and pulled up her long skirt. When she turned back to Sam she had Pearly's gun in her hand. "Here. Can you get out with this?"

Sam looked at the gun and then at Celia. He looked at her for a long time, at her dark, troubled face and worried eyes.

He got up and came over and made no attempt to take the gun. "I could," he said. "Only I won't."

"But you've got to!"

"No."

"But, Sam!" Celia's voice was pleading. "It's all you need, isn't it?"

Sam's face was a little tense with anger. "How will Lovejoy think I got the gun? He didn't search you like he would a man that would come to see me. He'll know you brought it. And the government wants me bad enough that all your dad's power won't keep you out of trouble. I won't take it."

"But you've got to. You've got to!"

Sam shook his head stubbornly. "I don't aim to drag you into this. It's my fight, my hard luck. Put that gun away now and listen to what I have to tell you."

Celia's face reflected hopelessness and anger but she said quietly, "What is it?"

Swiftly Sam began to recount the planting of the gold ore, but Celia interrupted him with the statement that Pearly had already told her.

"Then there's just one thing that will keep Santee from gettin' that right-of-way. As long as those jugheads out there on the Rio Medio think they'll find gold, they'll stay there. A boom camp grows fast and dies slow. And the only way it'll die quick is for George Harnum to spread the word it's a fake. Pearly's got to catch George before he gets back to the mine, and he's got to hold him. We got to keep that camp on the Rio Medio."

"But what good will it do?" Celia cried. "You'll be in jail. Pearly can't fight Santee alone. What difference does it make whether Santee gets the right-of-way tomorrow or next month? He'll get it, because you'll be in jail."

Sam smiled thinly, reflectively. "Let me see," he said. "I been in jail—well, let's say a dozen times in my life. I've broke out every time."

"But not this time, Sam. Not when the Governor wants you so bad that he signed his name to your reward dodger! And you were never accused before of killing the son of the most powerful man in the Territory!" She put her hands on the bars. "Please, please, Sam, take the gun and break out!"

"No."

"But won't you let me do even that to bring Steve's killer to justice? Because if you're out, you can catch Santee or kill him!"

Sam shook his head slowly. The muscles on his jaw corded with the effort to control himself. He would have given almost anything for that gun, for a last chance at freedom and Santee Bales. But he knew that as soon as he accepted the gun, Celia Drury would be in serious trouble. Matt Drury would never forgive his daughter. Lovejoy, with such evidence, would kick up a row that the Governor himself would have to take sides in. It could do something to this girl that she might never get over.

He said, "I never used a woman yet. Why start now?"

Celia was convinced that further argument was useless. She put the gun away under her dress, and when she turned to Sam again her face was gentle and her eyes luminous. "Well, I tried," she said.

Sam didn't say anything. Celia put out her hand, and Sam held it. "I'll do whatever I can to free you, Sam. You—you've been a friend."

Sam said softly, "So have you." He hesitated then, for what he was about to say was hard, and it deserved saying. "Once I said a lot of pretty bad things about you, remember?"

"Remember? I'll never forget them. They were true."

"I'm sorry I said them."

Celia smiled softly. "I'm not. They made the difference between existing and living. They hurt, and they were true, and I deserved them," She faltered a little. "I—said some things about you, too. Only where yours were true about me, mine weren't true about you."

"I'd even forgotten 'em."

"I'm sorry."

"That don't even—" Sam stopped. Tears were streaming down Celia's face, and she turned away from him and walked a few steps. Then she said, "Good-by, Sam. And God bless you."

She went out. Sam heard Lovejoy's embarrassed mumble, ending with, "He didn't confess, then?"

"No," Celia said, "he didn't confess." And she went out.

CHAPTER SIXTEEN

It was a long and weary ride to Santa Luz. They took him to McHarg, a stop on the northern stage route, and bought out every seat on the southbound stage. After filling it with the half-dozen Trabajo men whom Lovejoy had deputized, they continued the long ride to Santa Luz. Sam hoped that Pearly would not attempt to rescue him. The guards had been assured that they held the most dangerous man in the Territory; they were nervous enough to shoot first and ask questions afterward of anyone who tried to stop the stage. But Pearly made no such attempt, and Sam thought he could understand why. Pearly's mind just didn't run to fighting. Instead, he would be pleading with Matt Drury to use his influence in Sam's favor. No, if Sam got away it would have to be through his own efforts, and for the present he would have to put aside all thoughts of escape. A change of guards, men indifferent to the crimes of which he was accused, would be less wary, less dangerous. He slept most of the time.

They pulled into Santa Luz in the early morning, and Sam was taken from the stage to the Santa Luz jail, a large, twelve-cell affair in a corner of the one-story stone courthouse just off the plaza. He was given breakfast, then four men came in, handcuffed him again, led him out of the cell block and into the courtroom. He was arraigned there before a handful of loafers, and pleaded not guilty, through a lawyer furnished by the court, to the charge that he had murdered Stephen Drury. All through the hearing, Sam acted bored; his speech was lazy and curt, intentionally exasperating. Lovejoy, at the prosecuting attorney's questioning, explained young Drury's murder, presenting the evidence for the prosecution.

When the judge heard all the evidence, or enough of it to bind Sam, he said, "Samuel Teacher, do you plead guilty or not guilty to the charge?"

"What charge?" Sam demanded.

The judge leaned forward. "You weren't listening?"

"I heard some burros brayin'," Sam said mildly. "I didn't know they was in the room."

The judge, controlling himself with a visible effort, stated that since this was a murder charge bail was not allowed, and then said curtly, "Take him away. I presume he wants to plead not guilty."

"Suit yourself," Sam said.

The judge straightened up. "Did you say I could suit myself?"

Sam's lawyer said hurriedly, "He pleads not guilty, your honor."

"I'd like to hear him say it," the judge insisted.

"To hell with you," Sam said.

The judge stood up, about to speak, and then he checked himself. He looked down at Sam a long moment. "According to law, you are speaking through your attorney, who has entered a plea of not guilty to this court. This is the capital of the Territory, Teacher. We try to make our courts something of a model for others. But if I were in another court and not so punctilious, I would take you at your word. Your plea would be guilty. You would be sentenced to die and would hang within a week. Think that over the next time your arrogance runs away with you."

"There won't be any next time," the prosecuting attorney said.

"Exactly. And that gives me pleasure," the judge said. "Now take him away."

A deputy put a hand on Sam's arm; Sam shook it off. He swaggered down the aisle between his four guards. And then he stopped, his eyes on the knot of spectators sitting on the benches behind the rail. Shorty and Tex, Santee's two understrappers, were regarding him with bland delight on their faces.

"Well, well," Sam said. "Buzzards gatherin' already?"

Tex said, "It's rough, Sam. I cried myself to sleep last night."

"Out of a job?" Sam asked.

"Hell, no," Shorty said.

"You will be," Sam said. "Santee will be dead as soon as I get out of here."

"Oh, you gettin' out?" Tex asked.

"Inside a week."

The deputy shoved Sam along, and he grinned amiably at Tex and Shorty. "You boys watch out," he told them over his shoulder.

Back in the cell, the tedium of imprisonment settled down on him. Every moment he spent in here meant that Santee had that much better chance of getting the right-of-way. He looked about the cell block hopefully, but this was no small-town jail. Solid stone walls, four barred and screened windows, none of which was in his end cell, a stone floor, and a ceiling so high he could not reach it even by standing on his bed.

He lay back on his cot and rolled a cigarette and was about to light it when he heard the cell-block door open and a voice say, "Leave us alone."

Sam got up and saw the U.S. Commissioner approaching.

The Commissioner stopped before his cell and for several seconds did not speak. But his flushed face reflected that he was about to pour out a righteous man's indignation.

Sam spoke around his cigarette. "Get it over."

"I have talked with murderers before," the Commissioner said slowly. "They were usually sorry. You aren't even sorry."

"No."

The Commissioner sighed. "I came here to thank you

for one thing, and only one thing. The Governor's part in your scheme has not been brought to light. He is grateful."

"All right."

"I hope you can die with that small secret. It's not asking much, when you consider the Governor gave you your chance for freedom and a new life. Is it?"

"No."

"However, don't expect leniency. The Governor didn't ask me to make this request. I'm doing it on my own responsibility."

"All right."

The Commissioner looked steadily at him. "Of course, you understand that you'll hang. You not only committed a murder, but you killed the son of the Governor's best friend."

"Hurry it up," Sam said.

"I'm giving my personal attention to this. You'll get a fair trial. But I warn you, every crime you have committed—every murder, every robbery, every gun fight—will be used as evidence against you if I can so influence the court to admit that evidence."

Sam said, "Drag it."

"Not quite yet," the Commissioner said. "I want to express my own personal opinion of you. I'm speaking as a man, not a public servant."

"I know," Sam interrupted. "I'm a blot on the fair name of the Territory. I have shamed the mother who bore me. All the law officers of this Territory deserve a stern rebuke for lettin' me live this long. I am so cowardly, so low, so evil that I don't even deserve a trial. This is one case where every decent man longs for the good old days of Mexican torture, when a man was staked out on an ant heap, or when hot lead was poured down his throat. Right?"

"Exactly," the Commissioner said, putting on his hat and turning to go.

"Wait a minute," Sam said. The Commissioner halted.

"You know what I got to say to all that?"

"That we can all go to hell," the Commissioner said. "Isn't that it?"

"Exactly," Sam said, and raised his hand in a mock salute. He went over to his cot and lay down.

Dinner was brought by a big, surly guard who was unarmed, so that there would be no reason for overpowering him. Sam took a look at the food. It was a greasy beef stew, a thick wedge of bread, and a tin cup of muddy coffee.

"Take it away," he said.

"You'll eat it, mister," the guard said. "You know why?"

"No. Why?"

"Because you don't get no new stuff till you eat that. That's why."

Sam said, "All right," and didn't make a move toward the food. The guard placed it on the floor and went out. It was still there when he came in at nightfall. He took a look at it and said, "It's your own idea," and went out.

Sam was really hungry now. After the guard had gone, he went over to the tray and regarded it with distaste. This was a simple way of breaking a prisoner's rebellion, he reflected, and it was a good one. Nobody wanted to starve. He picked up the wedge of bread and broke it, and something dropped out of it, ringing on the floor. He picked it up and held it in the light of the overhead kerosene lamp, which burned in the corridor. It was four inches of a gun barrel. The sight and several inches had been hacksawed off to fit the wedge of bread which had been baked around it.

He contemplated it a long moment, his brow wrinkled in a scowl. His interest roused, he turned to the stew and stirred it with his finger. He felt something and fished it out. It was the butt plate of a six-gun. Turning to the cold coffee, he drank it and found mixed with the dregs six screws and a spring for a gun.

Squatting there, he pondered this. Was Pearly outside, trying to smuggle him a gun? Had he bribed the restaurant owner who was under contract to feed prisoners? If Pearly hadn't, someone else had. Celia? Or one of the many Mexicans here in Santa Luz whom he had befriended? A cold smile played on his face as he thought of it. From now on he couldn't refuse a meal for fear of missing parts of the gun. Then, with sudden panic, he realized that this was the noon meal he was eating, not the night one.

He wolfed down the bread and stew, gagging at its cold greasiness. Then with the tin coffee cup he beat on the floor until the guard came in.

"I ate this and I'm still hungry," he said. "Any chance of gettin' a meal tonight?"

The guard looked at the empty tray and said, "I reckon."

He took it out and within fifteen minutes came back with a meal which was identical, save that the stew was made with ham this time. When the guard left, Sam broke open the bread, as he had done before. A handful of small parts—bolts, screws, and the cylinder—fell out of the bread. The stew held the other butt plate, the coffee the ejector spring.

Sam hid them all under his mattress, then lay down, trying to still the excitement within him. It was long before he went to sleep. He was wakened in the early morning hours by the arrival of a drunken Mexican who was thrown into the cell across the way. When it was quiet again, he began to wonder. What if his tray of food was given to the Mexican in the morning? Could he argue the man into giving him the gun parts and keeping his mouth shut? He went to sleep again, wondering.

When the breakfast tray came in, he let the guard put it in his cell, pretending, indifference. The guard also left a tray in the cell of the Mexican, who was still sleeping.

As soon as the guard was gone, Sam lunged off his cot and examined the food. Yes, he had received the right tray; there were more parts. When he had finished eating, he drew out all the parts and took stock. He was lacking several screws, the hammer, and the frame. And some cartridges. Impatience ate at him all morning, and he smoked cigarette after cigarette. The Mexican wakened in midmorning, took a look at his food and refused to eat, and conversed idly with Sam. But Sam was uncommunicative, and the Mexican gave it up.

His dinner tray held a deep plate of bean soup. And in it was the frame. He looked up to see if the Mexican was watching him, and noticed that the Mexican was drinking soup, his face hidden by his plate. Sam switched the frame to the mattress, and then it occurred to him that the guard had not made the Mexican eat his breakfast. Maybe that punishment was reserved for long-term prisoners.

His night meal brought the hammer and a small screwdriver. In the bread were six cartridges and the missing screws. Darkness was long in coming, and Sam fretted with impatience until it came. Once the cell block was dark and only the overhead lamp threw out its feeble light, he went to work. His knowledge of guns was accurate enough that he had no trouble putting the six-gun together. The Mexican was asleep now, and he tested the gun time and again. It worked perfectly.

Slipping the cartridges into the chamber, he lay back on the cot and planned his next move. Should he call the guard in now on some pretext of getting tobacco or matches for him, or should he wait until morning and make his break then? The Mexican was asleep now. Maybe he wouldn't have to waken him.

He rose, thinking still about the Mexican, and his mind kept jogging back to the fact that the Mexican had not been made to eat his breakfast. That was strange. It was strange, too, that the guard had contrived to deliver the right tray to him each time. Could the guard be in on it?

Sam settled back on the cot, caution nagging him. He tried to remember the guard's actions, his looks, hunting for anything that had seemed suspicious. In order to deliver the right tray each time, the guard would have to be in on it. Then why hadn't he spoken? Why hadn't he just handed him a gun, instead of going through this elaborate pretense? There was something funny here.

He pulled out the gun and looked at it. The firing pin was not sawed off, and that was all that could keep the gun from firing. And then he thought of the shells. He took them out and examined them. They looked all right. Still, he couldn't be sure. He worked out the lead slug of one and then poured the powder out on his hand. It felt strangely cool. He went over to the light and looked at it.

It was flour.

He stared at it a long time, his mind piecing all this together. Whoever had sent that gun and the phony shells wanted him to make a break, thinking he had a loaded gun. Then, when it came time to use it, he would be a sitting duck for anyone else with a gun.

But who was it? There was only one man who would want him dead that way, and that was Santee. But Santee was— Ah! Shorty and Tex, Santee's men! Santee had probably got word to them to kill him before he could testify in court as to the true murderer of Steve Drury. They had chosen this way—and it had almost worked.

He settled back on the cot, his mind racing. Suddenly he came to a decision. He got the screwdriver and took off the two butt plates, then screwed them together. End to end they made a piece of solid metal about eight inches long. It was enough.

He settled down to the night's work of bringing the top of one butt plate to a point and then sharpening its edge on the rough stone of his cell.

It was tedious work, but by the first flush of dawn he had an imposing dagger with a four-inch blade, almost razor sharp.

Soon after sunrise they would bring his breakfast. He fought down the impatience raging inside him and waited.

When the guard opened the door, Sam made sure the gun, minus the butt plates, was in his waistband in the small of his back. The makeshift knife was in his hand, the point up his shirt sleeve.

The guard brought Sam's tray first. He looked carefully at Sam, and Sam knew that he was in on the scheme. Setting the tray down, he unlocked the door, then picked up the tray. Sam lunged to his feet, whipping the gun out with his left hand and pointing it at the guard.

"Steady," he said. "Put that tray down!"

The guard stooped slowly with the tray to put it on the floor, and Sam grinned as the man's hand moved to his boot top.

Sam stepped over and put the knife directly between the man's shoulder blades and bore down on it till he could feel it break the skin.

"Just one move, and this goes clear through your back. Put your hands out straight!"

The guard grunted and put his hands out.

"Now straighten up, and keep your hands up."

The guard did, and all the while the pressure on the knife did not slacken. Sam stooped then and flipped a six-gun out of the guard's boot top, cocked it, and pointed it at the guard.

"This one is loaded, I'll bet," he said.

The guard started to stammer something, and Sam cut in. "Who put you up to this? Who's in on it?"

"Two men. I dunno their names."

"Think," Sam said, jamming the gun in his ribs.

The guard opened his mouth to yell, and with a swift slashing movement Sam slugged him on the chin. He fell to the floor, unconscious.

Sam looked about him. The Mexican was still asleep; little noise had been made in disposing of the guard.

Sam flipped the gun loading gate open, made sure there were five shells in the cylinder, then started down the corridor on tiptoe.

Beyond the door, he remembered, there was an anteroom holding a table and several chairs. Beyond that was a corridor and at the end of that was the street door. He shouldn't have any trouble.

He opened the door confidently, the gun ahead of him, and stepped into the room. Tex and Shorty were sitting at the table playing cards. The sound of the door closing made them look up.

Sam said, "A little early for cards, ain't it? Waitin' for someone?"

Shorty looked at Tex and smiled. "Do you want him or shall I take him?"

"Just a minute, Shorty," Sam said. "Take a look at this gun."

Shorty's comprehension was slow. He was rising, his hand already swinging down to his gun, when Tex lunged across the table and grabbed his wrist.

Shorty glared at him. "What's the—"

"Look at that gun!" Tex snarled.

Shorty swiveled his head to look at Sam's gun. His face turned a dirty gray and he yanked his hand away from his gun butt.

"I thought that'd change your mind," Sam said gently. "Step inside, boys."

Under Sam's gun they filed into the cell block and he locked them in his own cell. Waving a lazy hand at them, he said, "I'll see you with Santee, boys," and went out through the anteroom into the corridor.

Out on the street, he had to walk a whole block before he turned into the empty plaza. Only a handful of horses were in sight. Their owners had probably made too good a night of it in the saloons.

Sam passed up the first three ponies because they didn't look like stayers. The fourth, a big chestnut in front of the Territorial Bar, he liked and took. Riding around the plaza, he saluted the sentry at the barracks and got a careless wave in answer.

He was a block past the barracks before he heard a gun go off in quick staccato. That would be the alarm; he lifted his horse into an easy lope.

CHAPTER SEVENTEEN

THE SEVEN MEN, including Sheriff Lovejoy, who had taken Sam to McHarg and put him on the stage for Santa Luz, passed Santee Bales less than ten miles out of Trabajo, although Santee pulled off in the brush and let them pass without making himself known.

Afterward he did not seem in any hurry. McHarg was thirty miles away from Trabajo, and if he kept his horse at a walk and lope, he could make it by the next noon. But at sunup he had breakfast with a Mexican in his humble adobe at a place considerably under the halfway mark. He ate his breakfast without haste, and did not speak during the whole meal. Afterward he paid for it and mounted and headed on again at the same leisurely pace.

Santee Bales was thinking. During the long ride that night he had cast up his score and it did not suit him. Sam Teacher was in jail for murder, but whether or not he would stay there long was a matter of conjecture. He had never stayed in any jail yet. When he got out of that jail, he would take up the trail where he had left off. And Santee did not like that. He knew since that affair at the dam that he might as well face the facts: he was afraid of Sam and he could not match him in a shoot-out. He simply didn't have the nerve. Granting those two points, which Santee reluctantly did, he decided he'd have to kill Sam before Sam killed him.

That was one question settled, the least of the two that were troubling him. The other question dealt with Drury and the right-of-way. As things stood now he could scarcely hope to get that right-of-way. A bit of bad luck, the twist of fortune which even the most careful man cannot forecast, had done him out of it. He might possibly get it in the end, but the chances were Sam would get him first.

That brought it down to cases. So far he had played this game with utmost care and skill, and Sam Teacher had shaded his every trick. But now that Sam was out of the way temporarily, Santee wondered if this wasn't the time to play his trump card. By late afternoon that day he had made up his mind that it was.

He rode into McHarg just at dark and immediately put up his horse in the livery stable. McHarg itself was a tiny cowtown of false-front stores flanking a rutted and dusty street. From the middle of the main street, a man could look in either direction and see where the sage flats took up as the last building left off.

Santee went immediately to the small hotel in the middle of the block. At his entrance a man rose and came over to him. It was Rhodes Latham, the foreman of Bales's ranch far to the south. Santee had sent for him from Santa Luz when he had got the court order, anticipating that he would have use for him and some of the crew.

He said, "Let's go up to your room."

"Want to eat first?" Rhodes asked.

Santee shook his head, and Rhodes led the way. Rhodes Latham was a Texan, lean, bleach-haired, pale-eyed. He was as tall as Santee, but he lacked Santee's barrel chest and rolling walk. By contrast he seemed indolent and lazy and deceptively mild.

Rhodes's room, the best the hotel could offer, was a tiny cubbyhole under the roof which still held the heat of the day.

Rhodes threw open the window, shut the door, propped a chair against it, waved Santee to the bed, and took the other chair, tilting it back against the wall.

"No catchum?" he finally asked.

Santee grimaced wryly. "They struck gold in the canyon."

"I saw them load Sam on the downstage this noon. He behind it?"

Santee shook his head, then asked, "Shorty and Tex in Santa Luz?"

Rhodes nodded.

"Have them get Sam, make a try for him anyway. I don't want him anywhere around when I pull this next job off."

Rhodes nodded acknowledgment of the order, but his interest lay in the second thing Santee had said. "What kind of a job?"

"A kidnaping for a seventy-five-thousand-dollar ransom."

Rhodes let his chair down gently and whistled. "You're shootin' pretty high, chief."

Santee laughed shortly. "I'm a gone goose if I don't. I aim to pick up a lot of money and jump this country for good. The right-of-way is lost."

"Who you goin' to kidnap?"

"Matt Drury's girl."

Rhodes's eyes narrowed shrewdly. "After gunnin' that boy of his?"

"That's right."

"Can you?"

"Getting her is easy. It's hiding her that's going to be tough. And that's going to depend on you and the boys. It'll take a lot of riding, maybe some shooting. But we got the whole Ute mountain range to hide in."

"You'll have the whole country after you."

"After *you,*" Santee said dryly. He shifted his weight on the bed and fixed a pillow behind him. "Rhodes, you and I have been together a long time. Have I shot square with you?"

"More than square."

"Would that ranch of mine be payment enough for risking your neck—and I mean really risking it?"

"Sure," Rhodes said immediately.

"All right. When that girl disappears, you're going to

take care of the posse. You're going to cloud my back trail so good that the whole country will chase you clean down to old Mexico—if you can stay alive to do it."

"I like that sort of game."

"I'm not holding out on you," Santee said quietly. "You got a fifty-fifty chance of getting away with it. But if you do, you got the deed to my ranch in your pocket, and it's yours, lock, stock, barrel, guts, feathers, and all. There's the proposition."

"Taken," Rhodes drawled.

Santee hove himself to a sitting position now. "All right. First, send a man down to Santa Luz with word to Shorty and Tex to get Sam. Next, you and four of the boys—Where are they, by the way?"

"Camped out on the flats."

"You tell four of the boys to drift over to this boom camp on the Rio Medio tomorrow and act like they've come to try their luck. They'll split up. When the hell pops, there'll be a posse formed out there, and they'll be in it. We'll know every move it makes."

"You still ain't told me my job."

"You drift into Trabajo tomorrow and get them used to seeing you. Keep your mouth shut, hang around the Chamisa saloon, and stay away from the Gem Café. I'll meet you there in a week."

"But the job," Rhodes prompted.

Santee shook his head. "I haven't thought it out yet." He stood up. "Better drift out and get the boys moving. Pick 'em careful, Rhodes, and tell them there's a stake in it for them when I swing it."

They went downstairs, Rhodes going out to the camp to give orders, Santee to get a room, after which he ate and went to bed.

A week later, Santee drifted into the Chamisa saloon in Trabajo, bought a drink, and in the bar mirror saw Rhodes seated in a chair against the wall by a poker table watching the game. When he was certain that Rhodes had seen him, he paid for his drink and left. Outside, in the darkness below the Chamisa, he waited until Rhodes came out, then he walked to the corner, turned right, and pulled up in the mouth of an alley.

Rhodes came past a minute later, and Santee murmured, "Here."

Once deep in its shadows, Santee said, "Leave anything at the hotel they can identify you by?"

Rhodes thought a minute and said, "No. I only left a razor."

"You won't need that," Santee said grimly. Then he outlined his plan, and Rhodes listened carefully. When Santee was finished, Rhodes said, "You're sure this freak shoe won't lame the pony?"

"No. I rode him for fourteen hours, day before yesterday." He paused. "Well, want to try it?"

"I'll need cash."

"Here's five hundred."

Rhodes took the money, put it in his pocket, and hoisted his pants. "Let's go," he said quietly.

"Give me half an hour," Santee said, and vanished down the alley.

Rhodes loafed about the darkened plaza for half an hour; then, the time up, he moved with decision. He went to the livery stable, got his horse, and headed for the alley that ran behind the Gem Café. True to what Santee had told him, there was a saddled horse tied to a shed just this side of the rear of the Gem Café.

Rhodes picked it up and stopped at the back door of the Gem and dismounted. Without knocking, he opened the door and peered in. Double-Jack was mixing up a great batch of dough on the big table in the center of the kitchen. The kitchen was warm and smelled of yeast, and big circles of perspiration dampened the back of Double-Jack's shirt.

"Come in," he growled, and Rhodes, acting like a shy puncher, stepped inside and closed the door.

"Miss Drury here?" he asked.

"Sure. What you want with her?"

"Her old man's sick."

Double-Jack paused, his hands in the dough up to his wrists. "Matt? Hell, he was in here this afternoon."

"I know it. He was took sudden."

"What is it?"

Rhodes shrugged.

Double-Jack took his hands from the dough, wiped them on his apron, and disappeared through the door that led to the front. In a moment he followed Celia Drury into the kitchen.

"You say Dad's sick?" She asked Rhodes.

"Yes'm. Nick sent me in to get you. I got a horse outside waitin'."

"Is it bad?"

"He didn't say, miss."

Celia went upstairs, came down in a moment wearing a divided skirt, and said, "All right."

Rhodes helped her into the saddle, then they turned up the alley, skirted the plaza, and headed out the road toward the Star 22.

Celia didn't talk much, but asked once, "Did you fetch the doctor?"

"Yes'm. 'Fore I got you."

"Aren't you a new hand?"

"Yes'm. One week."

Once on the flats, Celia lifted her horse into a long lope, and Rhodes kept even with her. They had ridden perhaps twenty minutes when ahead of them there appeared a light on the road.

As they drew closer, it appeared to be a team and buckboard coming toward them, a lantern on the floor of the buckboard.

It was then that Rhodes reached out and took hold of the bridle on Celia's horse. "Pull up a minute, miss."

"Why?"

"This may be some news from your dad."

Celia obeyed, and Rhodes dismounted and walked around to the left side of her horse. Celia was watching the approaching Buckboard. Suddenly she said, "That's not news from Dad. That's Santee Bales."

Rhodes reached up, grabbed her by the waist, and pulled her out of the saddle. It took all his wiry strength to hold her off the ground as she fought and kicked at him.

Santee, approaching, called, "Ready, Rhodes."

There was another man with Santee. He stood on the floor of the buckboard, and as the buckboard passed, he reached out and took Celia from Rhodes. The buckboard did not even stop.

Celia continued to fight, but the man pinned her arms to her sides, lifted her feet off the wagon bed, and sat her down abruptly. "Quiet now, miss. Nobody's goin' to hurt you."

Santee was standing up now, looking back at Rhodes. "Light a match and make sure, Rhodes. And good luck," he called.

Rhodes, without moving his feet, struck a match on his pants and in its flare examined the deep dust of the road. All that appeared to the observant eye were the tracks of a team and buckboard heading east without stopping. Also on the road appeared the tracks of a man, dismounted, by two horses. Satisfied, Rhodes blew out the match, put it in his pocket, went around to his own horse and mounted, then gathered in the reins of Celia's pony. He left the road a hundred yards beyond, heading south across country.

Santee, relieved when he saw the match go out, sat down and said, "Blow the lantern, Jim. Then put her up on the seat between us."

Celia, who had ceased fighting by now, said, "Where are you taking me?"

"A trip to the mountains," Santee drawled. "Nothing's going to hurt you if you'll be reasonable. Otherwise, we got to gag and tie you." Celia didn't answer, and Santee said, "You hear?"

"Yes."

"What'll it be?"

"Is Dad sick?"

"No. That was a trick to get you away from town."

"But you're taking me back."

Santee took a deep breath. "Listen, Miss Drury. I know what I'm doing. I asked you a question. You want to be gagged and tied, or don't you?"

"I do not."

"Then sit up here between us." Celia did. Santee went on: "We're going to go around the town by the back streets and go out across the bridge on the other side. If you open your mouth to yell, you'll get hit. You understand that?"

"I do," Celia said coldly. "This is a kidnaping, of course."

"That's right. Now you know everything. So sit calm and just watch us work it out."

Celia had no choice. She was a small figure wedged in between these two men, and she knew if she made one move to jump out they would forcibly stop her. Going down the hill into town, she made up her mind that she was going to yell if she saw anyone, whether she was hit or not.

But Santee had planned this carefully. He turned left at the first back street, and drove down it. Celia looked at the houses on each side of the street and they were all dark.

And then it came to her that yelling wouldn't do her any good. The whole town had moved to the Rio Medio, and there was no one to hear her.

They skirted the town, came out on the other side of the plaza, and headed for the bridge. Just as their horses stepped onto it, she heard a team approaching from the other end.

Before she could make a sound, the puncher on her other side clapped a rough hand over her mouth and put a heavy arm around her shoulder.

Under the weight of him, she could not move, and

when she tried to bite his hand she found it cupped away from her teeth.

She struggled, but made no movement; she yelled, but made no sound. The wagon passed them in the dark, and Santee said gravely, "Howdy," and got an equally grave "Howdy" in return. The man on her right did not take his hand off her mouth until they were well beyond the bridge out on the flats.

Santee only chuckled when Celia caught her breath.

"Take your arm off my shoulder!" she said.

"Well, now, I don't—"

"Take it off!" Santee snapped. The man obeyed quickly. No more was said for a long twenty minutes. Then Santee turned the buckboard off on a side road to the left. In another half hour they came to the shallow Rio Arriba. Santee drove the team into the creek and headed upstream.

It was rough going, for the rocky stream bed threatened to jolt the buckboard to pieces. Stubbornly, however, Santee clung to the river. The ride here in the river bed seemed interminable to Celia, but she knew that Santee was doing a careful job of covering his tracks.

It was three hours later when Santee pulled out of the river bed into a clump of cottonwoods where a campfire was burning dimly. Three men rolled out of blankets to welcome them. They were a rough-looking crew who went about their work as if they had already received instructions.

They unharnessed the team and turned them loose, but not before Celia saw the Star 22 brand on the horses. Then they built up a roaring fire, pushed the buckboard astride it, and let it burn. The harness followed the buckboard. Santee Bales was taking care to leave no evidence behind him. Afterward, eight horses were brought in from where they had been staked out. Six of them were saddled, the other two packed with grub.

Santee waited until the last fragment of the buckboard was burned, then he ordered his four men to mount. As

Celia saw the preparations she could not fight down her despair.

"Where are you taking me?" she asked Santee.

"Up in the Utes." Santee laughed. "So high and so far they'll never find you—even if they think to look."

CHAPTER EIGHTEEN

SAM DIDN'T KNOW that two posses took out after him from Santa Luz. One was composed mainly of citizens, all primed for a lynching. When, a mile from town on the main-traveled highway to Santa Luz they lost his tracks among several hundred others, they were stumped. Later, they scattered into the foothills of the mountains behind Santa Luz, figuring he would not return to his old haunts in the north. The Governor, when he heard of the break, knew better. He dispatched two platoons of blue-coated cavalrymen under the command of a lieutenant—under the command of the Commissioner. An Indian tracker went with them. The Governor wasn't going to let this break go unchallenged.

Sam's first move, of course, was to find Pearly and learn if he had seized George Harnum, the ore freighter. To that end he rode hard and steadily, stopping seldom for sleep. Arriving in late afternoon of the third day at the rim, he rode close enough to the canyon to make sure that the boom camp on the old Rio Medio was still there. Sudden relief flooded him at sight of it, for that meant Pearly had caught George Harnum before he could learn of the boom and declare it a fraud. Sam took a cattle trail up onto the rim, and as darkness fell was heading toward the foothills of the Utes.

Three hours later he rode into camp. A fire was burning in front of the cave, but there was nobody around. He dismounted, just as Pearly's voice from across the canyon yelled, "Sam!"

Sam wheeled in time to see Pearly leaping down the

slope in a torrent of rock and rubble. Pearly dropped his rifle and grabbed Sam's hand and beat him on the back and couldn't speak.

"Where's George?" Sam asked, when he had explained his presence.

The light went out of Pearly's old eyes, and his face settled into gravity. He said, "You hungry?"

"Sure. But where's George?"

"I couldn't git him," Pearly said. "As soon as Celia got the word to me, I started out. I nigh onto killed my horse, but I was too late, Sam. He'd been into camp an hour."

"Well, what happened?"

"Plenty. A couple of miners from the Giant Glorieta come down to the camp yesterday. They tried to tell that mob that their ore was a fake, but nobody'd believe them. They went back to get George, and just at dark tonight he rode into camp."

"You saw him?"

Pearly nodded gravely.

Sam stared into the fire, a wry scowl puckering his lips. He looked up at Pearly and shook his head slowly and finally smiled.

"There's only one thing to do, Pearly."

"Knock off Santee before he can get the river back?"

Sam nodded. "What are we waitin' for?"

"Nothin' but food," Pearly said grimly.

While they ate a hurried meal, Sam inquired about Santee. But Pearly had not seen him; events out here had kept him away from town. "But you never saw a buzzard get very far away from a carcass while there's still meat on the bones." Pearly said wryly. "He'll be around."

Sam thought of that eventual meeting with a surge of excitement. He'd have to move fast and take chances, for it would have to be done before Santee, with none to stop him, put the Rio Medio back in its old channel. That was all right, Sam thought; if need be he would walk into the crowded dining room of the hotel and goad Santee into a showdown—but it must come at once.

They ate quickly and afterward saddled up and headed for Trabajo, getting into town just at daylight. Evidently the news had not broken in town yet, for it was quietly asleep. The Gem Café held the only light in the town.

Pearly and Sam dismounted at the kitchen door, and Pearly went in first. Double-Jack, up early to bake his bread, was sitting at the kitchen table with a cup of coffee beside him, reading the *Territorial Enterprise.*

He looked at Pearly and said sourly, "The Big Bad Man of the Barrancas. What the hell do you want?" It was in keeping with the amiable feud between them which had lasted as long as Double-Jack was cook and Pearly a wagon boss at the Starr 22. Double-Jack's jaundiced glance took in Sam, too, but he only nodded at him. Double-Jack had the feeling that here was a man with whom it paid to be careful.

"Celia up?"

"She ain't even here. Listen, some day you're goin' to walk in here and find Lovejoy and a couple of U.S. marshals waitin' for you."

"Where is she?"

"Matt was took sick last night. One of the hands brought word last night and took her back with him."

Pearly frowned. "Bad sick?"

Double-Jack shrugged. Pearly asked for any information about Santee and Double-Jack said, "I dunno anything about him and I wouldn't tell you if I did. I don't want nothing to do with that scrap."

Pearly looked at Sam. "Celia will know about Santee." He added, a little embarrassed, "I'd kinda like to see what's the matter with Matt, too."

"Let's ride out," Sam suggested.

They left the Gem and pulled into the Star 22 an hour later. Breakfast was finished and work assigned for the day, Pearly said, judging from the amount of smoke issuing from the cookshack chimney and from the number of horses in the corral. They rode into the small plaza and Pearly went over to the office.

Nick Armbruster let out a whoop when he recognized Sam. He came out and shook hands with him. The Star 22 outfit was loyal to its owner, but that loyalty did not include sharing Drury's hatred for Sam Teacher. They had not forgotten, and Nick Armbruster especially, the long-needed beating which Sam had given young Steve Drury.

"What's the matter with Matt?" Pearly asked.

"Nothin'. Why?"

"Ain't he sick?"

"Not any. Who said so?"

Pearly glanced briefly at Sam and then back to Nick. "Ain't Celia out here?"

"Not unless she rode in last night and I didn't know it."

Pearly's voice was tinged with alarm. "You didn't send one of the boys in to get her last night?"

Nick looked blankly at Pearly and then at Sam. "What are you talkin' about?"

Pearly told him what Double-Jack had said. Without a word Nick left them, walking hurriedly toward the house. He returned in ten minutes with Matt Drury. When Drury laid eyes on Sam, he stopped, amazement on his lean face.

"You—escaped," he said in a quiet voice.

Sam nodded.

Drury put out his hand to Nick. "I haven't a gun, Nick. I'd like yours."

Pearly said quickly, "Matt, is it more important to try to gun Sam or to find out what's happened to Celia?"

Drury took his reluctant gaze from Sam's watchful face. "Now what is it you've been trying to tell Nick?" he asked Pearly.

Pearly repeated the story of Double-Jack's. When he was finished, Drury said, "I wasn't sick and nobody was sent to fetch her." He looked puzzled. "What's happened to her?"

"Maybe you better go to town and see," Sam suggested.

Drury had forgotten Sam's presence, let alone his anger.

"Saddle me a horse, Nick, and come along."

The four of them rode toward Trabajo, but when they came close to the town, Sam and Pearly, not daring to enter, pulled off the road and headed toward a clump of screening cottonwoods. Pearly had Drury's promise that he would tell them what he found.

It was a long hour's wait, and Pearly, impatience mastering him, walked over to the edge of the slope and stared down at the town. When he came back he told Sam that the news of the Rio Medio fraud must have broken, for wagons were swarming back into town. Neither of them was much impressed by this news, for the question of Celia's disappearance was uppermost in their minds.

When Matt Drury and Nick again appeared, they were walking their horses, studying the road. At Sam's and Pearly's approach, Nick pointed to the road.

"She started out on this road, and somebody was with her. The tracks in the alley back there match these here." He looked up at Pearly. "Double-Jack never seen this man before that claimed he'd been sent to get her."

For a long moment, Pearly didn't speak, and then he said, "You mean somebody's took her?"

It was Drury who said in a quiet voice, "It looks that way, Pearly." He straightened up, and when he spoke again his voice was more normal. "Let's see where they go."

The four of them, all animosity forgotten, rode abreast down the road, blotting out the tracks of the buckboard, reading the plain tale that lay in its dust. Drury pointed out that one of the horses had a left rear shoe with double cleats, something he had never seen before. Presently they came to the place where Rhodes Latham had dismounted, lifted Celia from her horse and, without letting her feet touch the ground, transferred her to Santee's buckboard.

"Tightened a cinch," Pearly observed, seeing only Latham's tracks.

"And Celia never suspected anything yet," Nick said. "She'd have made a break then."

"Let's go on," Drury urged.

A mile farther, the two horses swung off into the sage-stippled plain and headed south at a long, easy lope. When they had gone far enough to ascertain the direction, Drury pulled up. "We'd better organize a posse."

Sam sat motionless in his saddle, looking off over the rolling grama grass flats toward the south.

"Drury," he said slowly. "You get your mail this mornin'?"

Drury looked at him keenly. "I had a little more on my mind when I went into town than readin' a newspaper."

"You get it," Sam said.

Something in his voice made Drury come alert. "Why?"

"I dunno," Sam said. "I got a hunch there'll be a letter there."

"About Celia?"

Sam nodded, and turned his level gaze upon Drury. "Just how much money would you give to get your daughter back?"

"You know where she is?" Drury asked in a sharp voice.

"I didn't mean that. Answer my question. How much money would you give to get Celia back?"

"I–I don't know."

"Then you better start thinkin'," Sam said. "Because you're goin' to have to answer it."

"You mean you'll get her back if I'll pay you?"

Pearly said harshly, "He means go get your mail, Matt!"

Without another word, Drury wheeled his horse and led the way back to the road.

Pearly pulled up and said, "We'll be out at the ranch, Matt, if you want us," but Drury didn't answer, and Pearly doubted if he had heard.

When they were alone, Pearly was silent a long time. "Santee?" he asked finally.

"Let's wait and see," Sam said bleakly. They arrived at the Star 22 about noon. The crew was out, and only Pearly, Sam, and the blacksmith came to the cookshack when the triangle rang. None of them talked much; there was nothing to say. Sam tried to flog his weary brain into action, but the four days in the saddle and the sleepless night had fogged his mind. Besides, there was nothing to be done until Drury returned.

He half-dozed during the meal. Pearly became uneasy and urged him to ride out with a blanket and sleep somewhere where there was no chance of being captured. The Star 22, he pointed out, was a dubious sanctuary, what with Drury feeling the way he did. Sam disagreed and was stubborn. He wanted to see what Drury found in his mail.

But later, when he went to sleep in his chair, he agreed, upon waking, that he would turn in in the bunkhouse. Pearly was to wake him when Drury returned.

Pearly, who watched Sam fall into a bunk and go to sleep immediately, came out and sat on the bench alongside the bunkhouse. He was thinking of Celia, almost afraid to imagine what had happened to her. Any other thing you could fight, but not the stealing of a woman. He sat there thinking of Celia, about her childhood, remembering when she was a small girl. And presently he went to sleep.

When the blacksmith looked up from his work after lunch, he saw Pearly dozing, and smiled. He was still at work in the doorway a half hour later, when he glanced up to see Drury, six troopers in army blue, and the Commissioner from Santa Luz just dismounting in the plaza.

In the one helpless instant it took him to realize that these men were after Sam at the Governor's orders, he stood motionless. They were between him and the bunkhouse, and if he walked across the plaza to waken Sam, they would suspect him.

He took the only way out. He swung his sledge on the anvil with such violence that its clang was deafening. Pearly, asleep on the bench, roused to behold the army in front of him. He lunged to his feet, just as a trooper lined a six-gun at him and said, "Where is he?"

Pearly looked over at Drury.

"They're after Teacher, Pearly. You'd better tell them."

"He's gone," Pearly said.

Sam wasn't, but the clanging of the anvil had wakened him. He rolled out of the bunk, wide awake, and edged toward the window. Pearly, his hands raised, was in front of it, and in front of him were the troopers. Behind them the Commissioner and Drury had already dismounted, and Drury was saying, "Let's try the bunkhouse," in a weary, dead-sounding voice.

Sam knew that if he drew a gun on these troopers, he was a dead man. And if they captured him, Celia Drury would be left at Santee's mercy, for Sam now finally accepted what he had refused to think this morning.

The back window of the bunkhouse was open, Sam saw, and he made his decision. He raced across the room and dived at it, his arms folded above his head to tear the screen. As he cleared the sill, he heard a trooper's gun go off, and then he landed on his shoulder in the dirt outside.

He heard a trooper shout, "Around in back!"

Sam came to his feet looking around him. For seventy yards around the bunkhouse, the ground was free of underbrush. To get to a tree even, he would have to run the gantlet of the troopers' fire.

There was one course left, and he decided on it as soon as he thought of it. He scrambled back through the window, drew his gun, and ran for the door. Through the front window he could see the last soldier streaking for the rear of the building.

He raced out the door, just in time to see the Commissioner legging it for the rear of the building. At sight of him, the Commissioner tried to check his pace, clawing at the gun in the ornate holster at his side.

Sam shoved him, and Pearly, sensing Sam's move, leaped on the Commissioner's back and drove him to his knees in the dirt. Without pausing in his stride, Sam vaulted onto the Commissioner's horse and dug in his spurs, heading for the blacksmith shop.

"Pour it on, Sam!" the blacksmith shouted and immediately the first shot from the troopers, who had by now come back to the front of the bunkhouse, cracked out.

The slug creased the rump of Sam's horse, and he exploded forward around the corner of the shop. With the building between him and the soldiers, Sam weaved through the cottonwoods, jumped a ditch, crashed through a willow thicket, and found himself on the edge of the grass flats.

Leaning low over the neck of his horse, he made for the nearest clump of cedars. Once he achieved them, he made for the next clump. Here he turned in the saddle to watch his back trail. A quarter of a mile behind him, just breaking through the willow thicket, came the first of the troopers.

Pearly had probably stampeded their horses, delaying pursuit. But in jumping the Commissioner, Pearly had thrown his weight against the law. He would be held now for aiding a wanted man, and Pearly wouldn't care, Sam knew.

Pearly in jail, Celia kidnaped. Or was she? Sam didn't even know. He would have to find out if Drury had got a letter in the mail. He tried to remember if Drury's face, when he had got a fleeting glimpse of it through the window, gave any clue, but he could not.

When the first shot was followed by another, Sam knew he would have to settle down to business.

CHAPTER NINETEEN

By DARK, Sam had lost the soldiers. Part of it was thanks to the Commissioner's horse, a magnificent long-legged sorrel that was fat from grain and sleek with good care.

When Sam stopped to blow him in the early dark, he reflected on his next move. He had to find out about Celia, but now that Pearly was gone he had no way of finding out, unless he went to Double-Jack. And with the old caution, he voted against that. No, he'd have to see Pearly. And Pearly was very likely in the Trabajo jail at this moment.

Sam mounted and rode back toward Trabajo. Arriving in the early evening, he paused at the slope above town and pondered the activity. He could see the tents of the troops pitched in the plaza in two orderly rows. But there were few saddle horses at the tie rails and the whole town was lighted up. That probably meant that a posse was out on the trail of Celia's kidnaper.

Sam rode down the sloping road, keeping to the back streets. A block from the plaza he dismounted and tied his horse to a hitching post in front of a dark house, and made his way toward the plaza. He knew what he was about to do was dangerous, but the time for thinking of that was gone. He met only one person, a woman to whom he doffed his hat in the darkness, before he got to the alley that ran behind the jail and Pearly's saddle shop. He approached the jail with infinite caution, half fearing that he was walking into a trap. But there was no one there. The light from the single window high in the jail corridor cast a feeble beam into the alley.

He rolled a barrel from under the eaves spout of Pearly's

saddle shop to a spot under the corridor window and mounted it. He could see into the cell block, and his heart sank. The cells he could see were deserted. Still, the lantern was lighted, and that argued that there was someone inside.

"Pearly," he called softly.

From almost under his nose, in the end cell against the wall where the window was, Pearly answered, "Sam?"

"Yeah."

"Get away from here! They're tearin' up the country lookin' for you!"

"What happened to Celia?"

"Matt got the letter," Pearly said bitterly.

"What did it say?"

"Seventy-five thousand ransom."

"Tell it to me, quick as you can."

"Whoever wrote it give Matt three days to get the money and to prove that the posse couldn't catch him. Then there's an unarmed messenger supposed to take the northbound stage from McHarg at noon on the fourth day. The money is supposed to be in a package. You know that big clay dune they call the Tent just south of where you come down out of the Buffalo Grass Hills? It's about two days northeast from McHarg?"

"I know the place."

"The messenger is supposed to throw the money out of the stage when it gets on top of the clay dune."

"You can see every beef for fifteen miles from the dune! Don't the kidnaper know that?"

"Sure. He says if he can see anything except the stage he'll kill Celia."

"What else?"

"That's all."

"Has Drury got the money?"

"No. He's ridin' to Sand Forks tomorrow and McHarg the day after. Between this bank and them two he can scrape up the cash by mortgaging the ranch."

Sam was quiet for perhaps a minute. Finally Pearly said,

"You there, Sam?"

"I was just thinkin'," Sam said. "Any word about the camp at the Rio Medio?"

"It's pulled stakes," Pearly said. "Now git out of here, Sam."

"Nobody left out there?" Sam insisted.

"There ain't a soul and they burned the claim book. Harnum proved all the ore they found was from the Giant Glorieta."

Sam said, "Ah," quietly.

"What?"

"Where's Drury?"

"Out at the ranch with the Commissioner. The army brought along an Indian tracker that was supposed to take out after you, but he's leadin' the posse now. Half the town's gone with him. Now will you get out while you can?"

"Anybody after me?"

"Only them six that was at the ranch. But they will be, after that tracker gets back. Now you goin'?"

Sam said gently, "Pearly, you'll be out of that jail in six days or sooner. Can you stick it out?"

"I can stick it out a year if you can keep your hide from bein' nailed up and Celia gets back safe. Now clear out before they pull the damn town down on your ears!"

"So long," Sam said. "Six days. Remember, Pearly."

He left the alley cautiously, went back to his horse, and rode up the slope out of town, heading for the Star 22. Now there was something to work on. His mind kept going back to what Pearly had told him of the ransom delivery. It was a good way, he had to admit, and the man that received the money had a fair chance of getting away. Only he wouldn't. For that man, Sam was sure, was Santee Bales. Santee, balked by the gold strike in his effort to get the right-of-way through Rio Medio canyon, had shifted his attack. All that mattered to Santee was the money, and he would get it through the ransom. Sam had to smile when he thought of how close Santee had come to getting the right-of-way. If Santee had postponed his kidnaping for just one more night, he would have seen the Rio Medio strike fold up. Nobody would have contested his right to put the river back where it belonged, and once that was done he would have made his bargain with the railroad. Instead, he had let his greed drive him into a more dangerous business, and this time it looked as if it would betray him. This time could be the payoff.

Sam put these thoughts aside as he came in sight of the Star 22. He was a fool for doing this, but the memory of the Commissioner's visit to his cell in the Santa Luz jail still rankled. It was a little debt he wanted to square up.

He left the Commissioner's horse in the very willow thicket which had screened his escape that afternoon, and made his way through the cottonwood thicket toward the house. Skirting the bunkhouse and the plaza, he arrived at the door in the wall of the patio.

Cautiously he inched open the door and stepped through and closed it behind him. There was a lamp lighted in the dining room, but he could see through the open doors that it was empty. It was the light in the window of Drury's office that attracted his attention.

Approaching the doorway, he paused and put his ear to the door. The mumble of conversation came to him, and he drew his gun.

Slowly he turned the doorknob with his left hand, the gun in his right, and opened the door an inch. Through its crack he could see Drury seated in one of the deep chairs facing the fireplace. His back to the door, the Commissioner was also facing the fire, talking with Drury.

Sam opened the door the rest of the way and stepped inside. Drury, when he saw who it was, lunged to his feet and wheeled to the desk. Sam knew that he was after a gun, and if he got it he would use it. The Commissioner had not yet realized what had happened.

Sam took two steps that put him behind the Commissioner, prodded him to his feet with his gun, then stepped behind his thick body just as Drury found his gun and swung around to face the room with it leveled.

"Drop it," Sam said.

Drury hesitated.

"Go ahead," Sam jeered. "You may be able to put a bullet through him and hit me."

"Put it down, Drury!" the Commissioner said. Although he had not seen Sam, he recognized the voice.

Drury said in a thick voice, "I have come to the place where I'd sooner kill you than live, Teacher."

"Go ahead and shoot," Sam said again.

Drury dropped his gun on the desk and said, "What do you want?"

"Sit down where you were," Sam said. "It'll take a little while." He slipped the Commissioner's gun from its holster and said to him, "You, too."

Once they were seated, Sam stepped away from them and circled around to the fireplace where he could face them. His face held a cool arrogance that made the Commissioner flush with anger.

"That's a good horse you have, Commissioner."

The Commissioner said nothing, and Sam grinned at his discomfort. He shifted his glance to Drury. "You're goin' to pay seventy-five thousand for Celia's ransom?"

"I am."

"And mortgage the spread to get it?"

Drury said steadily, "I am. I haven't the cash."

Sam said, "You didn't know, maybe, that Colver, the Southwestern and Rio Grande agent, is still in Trabajo with cash in his pocket?"

"What's that got to do with me?"

"Plenty. Drury, that strike at the Rio Medio has folded up. Maybe you didn't know that."

"I– Yes."

"And that land, thanks to my divertin' the Rio Medio, is yours, not Santee Bales's."

"What are you driving at?"

"Colver wants the Rio Medio canyon for a right-of-way. You own it. He'll pay you seventy-five thousand for it.

There'll be no gold hunters to fight your title for it if you sell it to Colver before Santee Bales can blow out that dam. Doesn't that make sense?" He was talking to Drury but he was watching the Commissioner's face. Over its florid expanse washed a look of utter bewilderment.

"Don't you think that's a pretty smart idea, Commissioner?" Sam asked gently, an undertone of irony in his voice.

"Why—" The Commissioner coughed. "I wouldn't like to interfere in Drury's personal affairs."

"Still, this business over the railroad right-of-way has been misery," Sam said to Drury. "Get rid of it, Drury. And it means that you won't have to paper the Star Twenty-Two for the ransom money."

Drury's expression showed that this had not occurred to him before, and that the suggestion was welcome. The Commissioner watched Drury closely now and Sam smiled.

"The Governor might be pleased," Sam said slyly. "He's wanted a railroad in the Territory for a long time."

The Commissioner's glance whipped to Sam, and there was a pleading in it that gave Sam pleasure.

Drury looked up from the fire at Sam. "I'm wondering if you want to make that deal because then you'll be sure of my seventy-five thousand?"

For a moment, Sam stared at him uncomprehendingly. And then the soft smile faded from his lips. His face was white as he walked over close to Drury.

"Drury," he said in a taut voice, "you think I killed your son. I can take that, because you had the evidence of my gun to make you believe it. But if you tell me that I'm in on Celia's kidnapin', I'm goin' to let this gun off in your face!"

The violence of his anger startled even Drury. Plain bewilderment at the identity of Celia's kidnaper and hatred for Sam had made him say it. And he suddenly saw that he had never been closer to death. Yet he was a proud man, and a fair one.

He said quietly, "I won't say it. I didn't mean it, I

reckon." He watched Sam's thumb on the hammer of the gun not a foot from his face. Then he raised his glance to Sam's face.

"I thought you didn't care any more about her than you do the rest of the world."

"I care more about her than she'll ever know, Drury," Sam said quietly.

He stood there a minute, letting his anger ebb away. On the heels of it came a surprise at his own actions. He had been trapped into an anger that he had never felt before. Drury's accusation had touched a pride that he thought was impervious to any insult, and he wondered why. And suddenly he knew that what he had said came from his heart. He backed off and said in a low voice, "Don't call anyone for five minutes," and stepped out the door.

When Drury did call, it was for Nick to saddle his horse. Fifteen minutes later he was on his way to Colver, and the Commissioner, alone in the house and reflecting on what had just passed, wondered if he knew as much of the criminal mind as he thought he did. For here was a criminal, the worst in the Territory, keeping his word to the Governor, risking his life to make good a promise that the Commissioner thought he had never intended to keep in the first place.

CHAPTER TWENTY

SAM HAD THREE DAYS in which to lay the groundwork for his scheme. It had its drawbacks, the chief one of which was that it would very likely bring a fresh posse on his trail. There was nothing to do about that, however, except to make sure that he had shaken the one which would be after him when he stepped out of the Star 22.

He worked at it all night and during part of it he had the light of a new moon. The process of clouding his back trail received some loving care and attention; an Indian tracker was sure to be a good one. When he had satisfied himself, it was daylight and he was somewhere near the stage road that ran northeast from McHarg. After two hours' sleep, he set out to explore this road. It ran almost string-straight across a country of rolling hills stippled with stunted cedar until it met the rim some forty miles to the east of the Rio Medio Canyon. Once it achieved the rim, it continued northeast across the plain before the foothills. It was on this plain that the Tent and the Buffalo Grass Hills were located, miles before the road lifted into the Utes and crossed them.

The part of the road that interested him lay between the top of the rim and McHarg, and when he found what he wanted—a place where the road crossed a dry wash under big cottonwoods—it was time to sleep. He went far back off the road, off-saddled, staked out his horse, and slept from midmorning to midafternoon.

He wakened with excitement edging him. By his calculation, the ransom money had been on the stage out of McHarg some five hours now. That gave him time enough for what he wanted.

He was ravenously hungry, and he had no food, but it didn't matter. Mounting his horse, he rode over as far as the stage road, then off-saddled, threw the saddle in the roadside brush, and gave the Commissioner's horse a slap on the rump. Watching him go, Sam knew that he was burning his bridges behind him. If he failed now, there would be nothing to do but wait for the Indian tracker to bring the posse to him.

The hour before darkness he spent in selecting the tree he wanted. It was a big cottonwood with low branches, one of which leaned out over the stage road. He climbed it and tested the branch, found that it was big enough so that it did not sag under his weight; then he came back to the fork of the tree and squatted there. During the wait, he pulled out the Commissioner's gun and tested its heft and made sure it had five loads in it and then he put it back in his waistband. There was no need to test his own, which was in its holster.

The stage gave him ample warning when it came. By the time it had sloped into the sandy wash where its wheels sank into sand that slowed its speed, Sam was flat on his branch over the road where it tilted up to the plain again.

He heard the horses breathing hard, the driver cursing. The horses pulled under him and then the driver. Sam was so close to him that he could have reached down and lifted his hat, but he did not make a move until the driver was past him. Then he rolled off the branch, feet first, and landed lightly on all fours on the top of the stage behind the driver. The driver, whipping up the horses, did not hear him. Sam hunkered there motionless until the stage was on the flat again and the rumble of the wheels would cover what he was about to do.

He pulled his gun, eased forward, and jabbed it into the driver's back. The driver started and then his back grew stiff under the gun.

"Don't talk," Sam ordered in a low voice. "Can you hear me?"

The driver nodded.

"Then hand me them ribbons. Step wide of me, go to the back boot, and jump off. Make any more noise than you can help and I'll blow you off the damn thing. Now move!"

Sam reached out, took the reins, and the driver, with Sam's gun still in his back, climbed back on the stage top. Reins in one hand, the gun in the other, Sam knelt there covering him as he climbed down into the back boot. He looked at Sam once, then jumped. Sam saw him land, roll in the dust, and then the darkness blotted him out.

Holstering his gun, Sam slipped down into the seat, arranged the ribbons between his fingers, and then began to whistle softly. Whoever was down there with the money had not seen the change of drivers. Sam hoped that it wasn't Drury; in the showdown Drury would be against him.

The thing Sam feared now was the change of horses up the road at the stage station. He had seen the station, a lone adobe house in sight of the rim and almost surrounded by corrals. Would the station hostler be suspicious when he didn't stop? He had to take the chance, but it wasn't much of a chance, since there was only the lone house there, and the hostler, if he suspected foul play, would not be foolhardy enough to pursue the stage alone.

It was almost midnight when the lights of the house became visible over the long flats. Sam did not slacken the pace of his horses. On the ground, lighting up a circle of the hard-packed yard, Sam saw the hostler waiting with a team of horses. Another lantern out in the corrals showed that the other teams were harnessed ready to hitch up.

The pace of the stage did not lessen as Sam kept to the road. He raised his arm in a slow wave and called, "No load," and watched the silent hostler. The man did not move, only watched the stage until it disappeared in the night. If he was alarmed, it didn't show on his face or in his movements.

Hours afterward, the stage moved into the steep rim

pull. The road zigzagged its narrow way up the face of the rim. There were hairpin turns and cutbacks that took careful handling as the road mounted up and up. The horses labored doggedly, their breathing and the jolting creak of the stage the only sounds in the night.

The road, where it leveled off for the plain above, pulled out of wide canyon walls, then turned to the right to avoid the shoulder of rock which jutted up on the left. This left a big, flat, boulder-strewn area on the right of the road, between it and the rim edge.

It was when the horses pulled into the turn and leaned back off their collars in weariness that it happened. One moment it was still and peaceful, and in the next the very night seemed to explode in gunfire.

The lead team went down, and before the other horses could stampede and rear, the second team went to their knees.

And then the hail of lead which was coming from the boulders to the right of the road swung onto the swing team. It caught them just as they were fighting to free themselves of the harness, and they fell, too.

Sam held the ribbons and watched for the ten seconds that it happened. Almost without knowing it he counted the number of guns over in the boulders; it was three.

Then a voice hailed him out of the night. "Driver, step down! Be sure you aren't armed!"

Sam dropped the ribbons and climbed down. There was a kind of wild elation in his blood, for that voice he knew. Santee Bales.

"Get out of the stage, you!" Santee called next.

The man who got out of the stage was Nick Armbruster. He stepped down beside Sam, and Sam heard him catch his breath in surprise.

"Lie down when it starts, Nick," Sam whispered.

Then two men stepped out from behind the boulders; in the thin light of the moon he saw that they were Tex and Shorty.

When they were clear of the rocks, perhaps fifty feet

from him, Sam saw Shorty hesitate and he knew the time had come.

"Open the ball, boys, because here it is," Sam said, and Nick Armbruster, unarmed according to instructions, rolled under the stage.

Sam's hands streaked for his guns as he ran forward. He had the first shot; it was from the hip, and it caught Shorty standing and spun him off his feet as if something immense and invisible had hit him.

Tex was holding the rifle that he had used to kill the horses; he threw it to his shoulder in a kind of wild haste and then he seemed to realize that Life and Time and Sam Teacher were not going to allow him to sight it and he shot blindly and dropped the rifle and lunged for the nearest rock. He was stretched out in a kind of frantic clawing to get behind the rock when Sam's shot hit him. It caught him in the chest and it turned him half over, so that when he fell it was on his side. He rolled on his back and lifted his leg once and then lay still.

By now, Santee's shots were hammering out from a rock in the rear of the boulder field. They came wild and fast and panicked. Sam slipped to the ground behind Shorty's body, and then Santee quit shooting.

"Celia!" Sam called. "Celia! Where are you?"

Off to the east, from behind the tallest boulder, Celia called, "Sam!"

Sam laughed aloud. Santee was as far from Celia as he himself was. She was out of the line of fire.

"I'm coming, Santee!" Sam called.

"You make a move and I'll kill her!" Santee yelled back. "I have a sight on her now."

"Nick dragged me out of the way, Sam! Go ahead!" Celia called.

Santee cursed. Nick, gunless, had still performed nobly. Sam saw a movement behind a rock and he laid a shot at it. He saw the spark the slug made where it hit, just a few inches below the patch of black.

"Keep down, Santee," Sam said. "Here I come. You

listenin', Santee?"

"Let's split the money, Sam," Santee said. "Seventy-five thousand."

"I'm movin' to that rock ahead and to the left of me, Santee. If you want a shot, take it!"

Sam straightened and ran for the very rock he mentioned. Santee shot three times, and the last time Sam felt something whip through his boot top.

"Move back, Santee," he called.

"Sam. Listen to me! We got a fortune here to split."

"Here I come."

Sam ran for the next rock, a farther distance, but this time Santee did not shoot.

"Santee!" Sam called.

There was no answer.

"I'll turn over every boulder in this field, Santee, until I find you!" Sam called.

From farther back toward the rim Santee said, "I give up, Sam. I surrender."

Sam laughed. "I'm goin' to kill you, Santee." He paused, letting that sink in. "Nobody surrenders tonight. Here I come!"

He raced to another rock and did not even pause behind it but made for the shelter of the one ahead of it. Santee shot only once, as if he were resigned to waiting until he had a clean shot.

Sam crouched behind the rock and peered out. He could see the rim now, perhaps thirty yards away. Santee shot then, and Sam yanked back, stone dust in his eyes.

"That's better, Santee," Sam said. "You want to stand up and shoot it out?"

Santee didn't answer for a long moment, and Sam loaded both guns.

"All right," Santee said, his voice strident. "You stand up first."

"Not me, Santee," Sam said. "If I stand up first, you'll shoot. But if you stand up first, you know I won't shoot. I don't have to, Santee. I can kill you with an even break."

"Go to hell!" Santee snarled.

Even while he was talking, Sam lunged out for the rock ahead of him. He crouched so close to the ground that he tripped and lost his balance. He heard a shot and felt something hot rake his back and he pulled up behind the rock, sprawled on his face. He got to his knees. The rim was only twenty yards away now. Santee was behind the biggest of the two rocks between him and the rim, and that rock was a bare six feet from the edge.

"How does it feel, Santee?" Sam called.

"Listen, Sam." Santee's voice was pleading, frantic. "I'll leave the country—give you all the money I've got—I'll do anything!"

Sam said nothing.

"I got a hundred and fifty thousand, Sam, countin' this seventy-five in the stage!"

Still Sam said nothing.

"You listenin', Sam?"

"You through?" Sam said then. "Because if you are, I'm comin', Santee."

Santee started to curse, his voice high and wild. Sam took a grip on both guns, and looked out at Santee's rock. Santee was not looking out.

Sam crouched, then exploded out of his hiding spot, both guns hammering. Santee came up shooting and running, running for the shelter of the other rock.

Sam let him take two steps, and then he swung his guns in a slow arc, firing. Santee swerved, stumbled toward the rim and caught himself. He pulled up and swung around, a gun in each hand. Then Sam stopped and shot once with each gun. At each shot, Santee rose higher, his head coming up. Then he did a graceful pivot toward the rim, his knees buckled, and he fell. There was nothing but space under him for three hundred feet.

Sam turned away and lowered his guns. Celia Drury was running through the boulders toward him.

CHAPTER TWENTY-ONE

THE SHERIFF'S OFFICE, by an unspoken agreement, was the center where everybody who was interested in Celia Drury's safety collected. Perhaps it was because Matt Drury, in these hours of agonized waiting, sought the company of the oldest friend he had, Pearly Gates. The Commissioner, the Lieutenant, Lovejoy, and Drury kept to the office, not talking much to each other. Out in the plaza the troops, returned from two fruitless searches, loafed around and waited, and the town was quiet and expectant.

It was like this when Sam, Celia, and Nick Armbruster rode in on the horses of Santee and his men, turned the corner, and pulled up in front of the sheriff's office.

Drury broke out of the office first and Celia swung out of the saddle and was in his arms. For a long moment they said nothing to each other, unable to speak.

The silence was broken by the sound of a gun being cocked. Sam looked up to see the Commissioner's gun covering him.

Drury said, "Thank God, honey, you're safe!"

Celia said, "Of course I am, Dad." She pulled away from him and looked at Sam. "Turn around, Dad, and see the reason why I'm safe."

Drury looked at Sam, and then at Celia, and then he said humbly, "Thank you for my daughter's life. But I don't understand."

Celia looked at the gathering crowd and said, "Can't we go into the office, Dad?"

As soon as Sam was dismounted the Commissioner stepped over and took his guns, and Sam did not object.

With the others, he stepped into the sheriff's office, and Lovejoy shut the door.

Celia was holding her father's hand, and when she saw them all looking at her she laughed a little shakily. "It wasn't bad," she said. "I was scared, I guess, at the last."

"Who was it?"

"Santee Bales." She paused, the memory of the past four days darkening her eyes. "He's dead."

Sam leaned against the wall, his face wary and faintly embarrassed as Celia told of the fight on the rim.

When she was finished, the Commissioner cleared his throat. "That took nerve, Miss Drury. Still, it was the nerve of a murderer, even if he did save you."

Celia's eyes flashed. "You mean that he murdered my brother?"

"He did. I—I'm sorry to have to say it."

"Then don't say it!" Celia cried. "Those three men dead at the rim are Steve's murderers!"

"How do you know?"

"Because those two, Shorty and Tex, talked about it in front of me while Bales was asleep."

A quiet smile creased Sam's face. "Sorry to disappoint you, Commissioner. You hoped it was me, didn't you?"

The Commissioner turned to look at Sam. "I did not," he said quietly. "Last night I began to hope I was wrong about you. But that murder was something I could not forgive." He smiled now. "I *was* wrong about you, and I admit it here and now." He crossed over to Sam and put out his hand. "I'd like to eat my crow in public. That amnesty still stands, Teacher, and we'll call all the reward posters in. I can speak for the Governor in that. And I speak for myself when I say I would like to shake your hand."

Sam's face thawed out gradually and he put out his hand. "I—I guess I was kind of rough on you."

"You were. About as rough as I deserved."

They shook hands then, the Commissioner and Sam Teacher.

"What about Pearly? He broke me out of jail and spoiled that capture yesterday," Sam said.

"You can't imprison a man for rescuing an innocent man, can you? Let's free him now."

The others went into the cell block, leaving Celia and Sam alone. She stepped over to the door and bolted it.

"You'll get hell for that," Sam said quietly.

"I don't care." She hesitated. "What are you going to do now, Sam?"

"I'll drift."

She looked at him. "Why should you do that?"

Sam's curiosity quickened. "You want me to stay?"

"What if I did?"

The alertness went out of Sam's face. "Nothing, nothing," he said. "Only, well—I—"

"Say it, Sam," she said in a low voice.

"I reckon not," Sam said. "I've been outside the law, Celia, and chances are I always will be. Only"—he looked at her gravely—"you're just a copy of me in skirts, Celia. You were wild and cocky, like me. And I saw you tame yourself, turn into a person folks can't help but like. Well—I—" His voice died.

She wouldn't help him. At last he went on. "I thought kind of that we should stay knowin' each other. Like, well—"

"Sam," she said gently, and walked over to him. "Are you trying to tell me you love me?"

"Yes," Sam said. "Yes, I am."

"Then why don't you say so? I love you, Sam. I want to be near you all my life."

Sam reached for her. The pounding on the door roused them, and Celia, holding Sam's hand, opened it.

Pearly was first out. He took one look at Celia and Sam and then turned to Drury. "You feel old enough to retire, Matt, and let me work for a younger man?" He looked at Celia. "You've found your man, I guess."

"That's it," Celia said, looking at her father.

Matthew Drury looked at Celia and then at Sam and his

glance lingered on Sam the longest. "Pearly has worn out one boss, boy. You want to give him a chance at the second?"

Sam Teacher said, "I do."

Later, Celia Drury said it, too.